THE STAR OF LOVE

In the past he had kissed many women. Too many, perhaps. But this was unlike anything he had experienced before. This was the kiss he had been waiting for all his life. The kiss of the one and only woman.

He felt her body soft against his and pulled her closer still, feeling that they were part of each other.

"Cliona," he murmured, kissing her again and again.

At last he drew back a little to look down on her sweet face, half expecting her to berate him for his forwardness. No gentleman kissed a girl so passionately on such short acquaintance. He had proved himself a cad – that was what she would say. Then she would slap his face. And he would deserve it.

He even hoped that she would do so and startle him out of the spell in which he was helpless to do anything but pursue her like a man pursuing a pixie light through a forest.

The Barbara Cartland Pink Collection

Titles in this series

THE STAR OF LOVE

BARBARA CARTLAND

Barbaracartland.com Ltd

THE BARBARA CARTLAND PINK COLLECTION

Barbara Cartland was the most prolific bestselling author in the history of the world. She was frequently in the Guinness Book of Records for writing more books in a year than any other living author. In fact her most amazing literary feat was when her publishers asked for more Barbara Cartland romances, she doubled her output from 10 books a year to over 20 books a year, when she was 77.

She went on writing continuously at this rate for 20 years and wrote her last book at the age of 97, thus completing 400 books between the ages of 77 and 97.

Her publishers finally could not keep up with this phenomenal output, so at her death she left 160 unpublished manuscripts, something again that no other author has ever achieved.

Now the exciting news is that these 160 original unpublished Barbara Cartland books are ready for publication and they will be published by Barbaracartland.com exclusively on the internet, as the web is the best possible way to reach so many Barbara Cartland readers around the world.

The 160 books will be published monthly and will be numbered in sequence.

The series is called the Pink Collection as a tribute to Barbara Cartland whose favourite colour was pink and it became very much her trademark over the years.

The Barbara Cartland Pink Collection is published only on the internet. Log on to www.barbaracartland.com to find out how you can purchase the books monthly as they are published, and take out a subscription that will ensure that all subsequent editions are delivered to you by mail order to your home.

If you do not have access to a computer you can write for information about the Pink Collection to the following address :

Barbara Cartland.com Ltd.
240 High Road,
Harrow Weald,
Harrow HA3 7BB
United Kingdom.

Telephone & fax: +44 (0)20 8863 2520

THE LATE DAME BARBARA CARTLAND

Barbara Cartland who sadly died in May 2000 at the age of nearly 99 was the world's most famous romantic novelist who wrote 723 books in her lifetime with worldwide sales of over 1 billion copies and her books were translated into 36 different languages.

As well as romantic novels, she wrote historical biographies, 6 autobiographies, theatrical plays, books of advice on life, love, vitamins and cookery. She also found time to be a political speaker and television and radio personality.

She wrote her first book at the age of 21 and this was called *Jigsaw*. It became an immediate bestseller and sold 100,000 copies in hardback and was translated into 6 different languages. She wrote continuously throughout her life, writing bestsellers for an astonishing 76 years. Her books have always been immensely popular in the United States, where in 1976 her current books were at numbers 1 & 2 in the B. Dalton bestsellers list, a feat never achieved before or since by any author.

Barbara Cartland became a legend in her own lifetime and will be best remembered for her wonderful romantic novels, so loved by her millions of readers throughout the world.

Her books will always be treasured for their moral message, her pure and innocent heroines, her good looking and dashing heroes and above all her belief that the power of love is more important than anything else in everyone's life.

"Never give up on love. It could be waiting for you just around the corner."

Barbara Cartland

CHAPTER ONE
1864

"Damn you to hell! Do you hear me!"

Over the desk one pair of blazingly angry eyes met another pair, cold but no less angry. The man with the blazing eyes backed off first, swinging away to move into the large bay window and stand with his back to the other man.

"Damn you!" he repeated in a more controlled tone. "You are a smug hypocrite and you don't even have the honesty to admit that you hate me."

The man behind the desk shrugged wearily.

"Would admitting it make any difference, John?"

"It would be honest. Why not just say that I'm a thorn in your flesh and that your world would be a brighter place if I died tomorrow – or preferably today?"

Charles Baxter, tenth Earl of Hartley, thought for a moment before saying quietly, "in other words, you'd like me to behave as badly as you do yourself?"

His cousin, the Honourable John Baxter swung round from the window as he faced his cousin across the elegant desk where the Earl kept his papers.

"You could never behave as badly as I do, cousin," he sneered. "You haven't the gift for it. Behaving really badly

1

is an art, one in which our family used to excel. By Jove, at one time this family made its mark. We could out-drink, out-ride and out-wench anyone in the county."

"And you regard that as something to be proud of?" the Earl asked, and this time his eyes were really cold.

"Oh stop being so sanctimonious! It was a triumph. It was how a great family was expected to behave."

"Yes, as though you were above the law, and oblivious to anyone else's wishes or needs. You call that greatness? I call it contemptible."

"The Hartleys were Titans, and the world knew it. But now? Look at us! You've become a virtuous prig and there's only me to keep the glorious traditions going."

The two cousins might have come out of the same mould, so alike were they. Both in their thirties, both six foot tall, long of leg and broad of shoulder, both with dark hair and eyes of deep brown.

Their faces too had been alike at birth, but John's already showed the effects of dissipation. A ceaseless round of pleasure and idleness had blurred his once sharp features, and a nature in which petulance and selfishness had conquered all else had left a discontented droop to his mouth.

His frame too bore the signs of self-indulgence in a thickening of the waist that even the most expensive cut to his coats could no longer hide. A man once called 'as handsome as a young God' was beginning to look more like a satyr.

By contrast, the Earl still had the lean, upright figure that spoke of country pursuits, long hours in the saddle and vigorous exercise. He both ate and drank in moderation and the contours of his face were still youthful, something that seemed to drive his cousin John into paroxysms of rage.

John was indeed in a temper now, caused by the Earl's

refusal to pay a huge debt that he had carelessly tossed to him.

It had arrived in the post three days ago, as so many had done before it. And Charles had promptly sent it back.

The response had come quickly. John had come raging up to Hartley Castle and stormed into the library.

"What the devil do you mean by sending these back to me?" he shouted, tossing the bills onto the desk.

"My letter means exactly what it says," Charles had replied. "I've paid too many of your debts in the past and this time I'm refusing."

"You always refuse, in the beginning," John had replied with the air of sneering assurance that was common with him. "And you always yield in the end."

"This time I shall not."

"You always say that, too."

"Listen John, I have other claims on me. As head of the family – "

"But are you, I wonder?"

Charles ignored this remark. He had heard the story too often before, and knew that responding always led to a fruitless conversation going round in circles.

"I'm responsible for the welfare of many of our relatives," he continued. "Too often I've put your gambling debts ahead of their needs."

"And you'll do it again unless you want a nasty scandal," said John, as Charles knew he would say. "How the newspapers would love to be able to print, 'Hartley heir imprisoned for debt'!"

"You've blackmailed me too often with that threat," Charles responded in a measured tone that showed he was trying to keep his temper. "This time I shall not allow it. The answer is no."

"How you enjoyed saying that!" John had snapped.

"It gives me no pleasure."

"Liar! It gives you every pleasure, because you hate me. *Admit it, you hate me!*"

But this admission Charles steadfastly refused to give, even though it came closer to the truth than he cared to face. There had once been a good deal of affection between them, and although it had long been replaced by hostility on one side and weary exasperation on the other, the memory of that affection kept him from any open admission.

Not receiving the answer he demanded, John stormed across to the window, hurling the word 'hypocrite' over his shoulder.

Still Charles refused to be provoked and John began to wander around the great library, staring up at the shelves that climbed right to the ceiling, row on row of leather bound books that few Hartleys (according to Charles) had ever bothered to read.

The library was a combination of shabby grandeur and comfort. Leather sofas and armchairs, worn rugs, a huge fireplace, empty now that it was summer, but in winter sporting a blaze to warm the heart as well as the hands.

Where the walls were not covered with books, there were many sporting prints and trophies. It was the library of a gentleman, an Earl, and a man who loved his country pursuits. And every inch of it seemed to fuel John's anger.

"I won't accept your refusal," he snapped.

"It is useless continuing this conversation," said Charles. "I have told you a thousand times that your extravagant way of life must stop."

"And I have told you a thousand times to go to the devil! It gives me great pleasure to tell you so again."

"John, you can't go on spending money that isn't yours."

"Why not?"

"Because you impoverish others who have a greater claim on it."

"Nobody has a greater claim than I," John shouted. "And you know why."

"Let us not go into that again – "

"Because you're afraid," John sneered. "You're afraid to bring the truth out into the open, afraid of the world knowing that it is I, not you, who is the true Earl of Hartley – "

"You have taken leave of your senses," said Charles in disgust. "This particular 'truth' is one you've been peddling for years to anyone who'll listen and your father before you. And nobody has yet believed you. Why should I be afraid if you say it again?

"Go ahead, John. Tell the world that our fathers were twins, and that your father was truly the elder son, but a drunken midwife muddled them. That's the story isn't it? Tell anyone you like but don't tell me, because like the rest of the neighbourhood, I know it isn't true and I'm bored with it."

A lesser man would have quailed before the malevolence in John's eyes. He truly could be said to hate his cousin.

"How do you know it isn't true?" he demanded viciously.

"For one thing because our grandmother has always dismissed the story as nonsense. Good heavens John, our fathers were her babies. Who could know the truth better than she? She's told you time without number to forget this myth, just as she told your father."

"She's lying," John said feverishly. "She's against me too. You all are."

"If people are against you, it's because of your behaviour. You lie, you cheat, you seduce women, you spend money you don't have and others suffer – "

He wasn't allowed to finish. Slamming his hand down on the pile of bills on the desk, John shrieked,

"Will you pay these?"

"No," said Charles bleakly. "I will not."

"By God!" John breathed, "I won't stand for this."

"I'm afraid you'll have to."

The Earl's voice was final, and it drove his already maddened cousin into a frenzy. Slipping his hand into an inner coat pocket, he pulled out a small pistol and held it to his cousin's head.

"Don't drive me too far," he gasped.

Perhaps a wise man would have placated John at that moment, but there was in Charles a vein of stubbornness that was like granite. It made him shrug his shoulders, even while he could feel the cold steel against his forehead and said,

"I don't respond to threats, you ought to know that by now. The answer is still no.".

"I'm warning you – "

"Don't warn me. I'm not impressed. Either fire that thing or put it away."

"If I fire you'll be sorry."

"No, I won't because I'll be dead. *You'll* be sorry because you'll be arrested for murder, but it won't trouble me one way or the other."

Charles regarded his cousin with a hint of amusement. "You wouldn't get away with it, you know. Everyone knows you're here, and you're my heir, and you're the first person they'll think of. Still, it would solve your debt problems, I can see that."

John breathed hard. "You dare to torment a desperate man?"

"For pity's sake, stop talking melodramatic rubbish!" Charles said, irritated to the point of tempting fate.

Whether his gamble would have resulted in tragedy they were never to know. For the next moment the door opened and Watkins, the butler, entered and saw John holding the pistol to Charles's head.

"Mr. John, sir!" he exclaimed horrified.

Watkins had known them both as boys and no dramatic atmosphere could survive his fatherly intervention.

The intent drained out of John's face and he took a step back, lowering his arm.

"To the devil with both of you!" he said angrily.

"It was only a joke, Watkins," Charles soothed him. "You know how incorrigible we both are." His smile at John was an invitation to return, at least for a moment, to their childhood friendship. "You don't think that thing is loaded, surely?"

It was a fatal thing to say, as he knew the moment the words were uttered. After that John had no choice but to pull out the pistol again, take swift aim at a china figure on the mantel piece and shatter it to fragments with a bull's eye.

"Now you know better," he said and stalked out.

"My Lord," Watkins said, pale and shaking. "I never was so shocked."

"Don't make too much of it, old friend," Charles said kindly. "You know him. It was all play acting. He wouldn't really have fired at me, you know."

"Not meaning to, perhaps. But with his finger shaking on that trigger, can you be sure what might have happened?"

"I suppose not," Charles agreed. He gave a rueful smile that made his rather stern face charming. "I was mad to defy him, wasn't I? I suppose in my own way I'm just as rash as he is. But I will not be bullied, even by a pistol."

He rubbed a hand over his tired eyes.

"Forget about it Watkins," he begged. "It was a passing mood."

"If your Lordship says so," the butler said woodenly.

The Earl grimaced. "Not much escapes you, does it? After all the years you've worked for us, does this family have any secrets left?"

"Not where Mr. John is concerned, my Lord. And I hope I do not need to assure your Lordship that I have never discussed family secrets."

"Of course you don't need to tell me that, Watkins. Although I imagine the worst is known fairly widely."

"I have heard gossip in *The Dancing Footman*," Watkins agreed, adding with a haughty sniff, "I discourage it firmly."

"Good man. And of course there is no need to trouble my mother and grandmother with this story."

"My lips are sealed, my Lord."

"I've told my cousin I won't pay another penny."

"Yes, my Lord."

"No matter how much he threatens me with scandal."

"No, my Lord."

"I know I've said it before, but this time I mean it."

"Yes, my Lord."

"And that's final."

"Yes, my Lord."

"And don't just stand there pretending to agree with me," the Earl said wrathfully, "when you know you expect me to yield, as I have in the past."

Thus appealed to, Watkins merely gave a shrug full of helpless sympathy.

The Earl sighed.

"I know," he said. "What's worse, *he* knows. That's why he's left the bills behind."

*

"My darling girl!" Lady Arnfield descended on her niece, arms wide, and enveloped her in a warm embrace. "Welcome, welcome!"

Lady Cliona eagerly hugged her back.

"Dear aunt," she said. "I have so much looked forward to coming to visit you."

The two women stood back to gaze on each other. Lady Arnfield was in her fifties, with a tendency to dress slightly too young for her age. The large crinolines that were the current fashion did not flatter her plump figure, and her love of extravagant decoration flattered it even less. But her manner was sunny and her face merry and kind.

The young woman smiling back at her was nineteen and had the slim, elegant figure to set off her fashion to perfection. Her waist was tiny, so were the little feet that peeped out from under her crinoline. Her face was pretty and full of mischief, and with her shining golden hair she at first might have given the impression of a charming doll.

It was her eyes that belied that impression. They were blue, almost violet, and they had depths that seemed designed to lure a man in to seek out the soul that resided there.

Part of her attraction was the fact that she seemed unaware of her charms. In a hectic London season she had flirted and laughed with her many admirers, but there was an instinctive simplicity and truth about her that drew as many men as her beauty.

But just now her aunt was chiefly concerned with pleasurable thoughts about what a sensation her niece was going to make in the neighbourhood. Few debutantes had enjoyed the roaring success of Lady Cliona. Prospective husbands had flocked to her, attracted as much by her charm as by her fortune, but Cliona had refused them all.

Now that the season was over, Lady Arnfield had plans for her niece.

The first stage of those plans consisted of taking her up to her room, and exclaiming with joy as Lady Cliona's maid unpacked her trunks.

There were piles of delicate underwear, embroidered petticoats, stockings, scarves, frilly handkerchiefs. There were dresses for the morning, dresses for the afternoon and dresses for the evening in satin, silk and lace.

There were tea gowns and promenade gowns, and riding habits, and riding boots and shoes for every occasion. There were necklaces and tiaras and rings and brooches and ear rings.

Lady Arnfield lived comfortably, for her husband was Sir Kenton Arnfield, Lord Lieutenant of the county. But they did not possess one third of Cliona's fortune and she had never seen anything like this wardrobe.

"My aunt Julia, who sponsored my London season, thought I was rather a spendthrift, I fear," admitted Cliona. "As you know, I didn't complete the whole season because I didn't reach London until May, and she wasn't sure I would need all of these clothes."

"Wasn't she indeed?" said Lady Arnfield, in a voice that boded ill for her sister Julia. "Well she never did have any sense of the right way of doing things."

"And I'm afraid she was further shocked when I bought more new clothes only last week," said Cliona with a face full of demure mischief. "She said such extravagance was quite unnecessary for the country."

"Then she's a fool," said Lady Arnfield. "And when I see her I shall tell her so."

Cliona began to dance about the room as though the train journey from London had not tired her at all. Which, indeed, was the truth.

"What a lovely room," she said, spreading her arms, turning and turning like a top.

"Goodness child, you'll be giddy," her aunt exclaimed.

"Dear Aunt Martha, of course I won't. At a ball I dance and dance all night without getting giddy."

"They say you were the belle of the season," sighed her aunt. "Admirers galore, and too many proposals to count."

"Naturally," said Cliona in a teasing voice. "Dear aunt, a girl with money always gets proposals. It's a tribute to her bank balance, not to herself, and she's a great ninny if she imagines otherwise."

"Oh, but I'm sure some of them must have been in love with you," countered Lady Arnfield, shocked by this unmaidenly realism.

"After ten minutes?" Cliona asked irrepressibly. "That was my fastest proposal yet. I can't tell you how conceited it made me. Think how I was brought down by the discovery that my swain betrothed himself to another heiress the next day. I was merely the first on his list, you see."

"Cliona!"

"Don't be shocked, dear aunt. What would you have me do? Believe that I really was the most beautiful, ravishing female the world has ever known? A paragon of virtue and delight – "

"I think I'm going to be ill," Lady Arnfield said frankly.

11

"That's precisely how I felt."

"Men really talk to you like that?"

"Some do. And it's fatal because I simply cannot bear having my intelligence insulted. Imagine how conceited I would be if I believed all that nonsense!"

"It doesn't bear thinking about," Lady Arnfield agreed.

"Sometimes," Cliona mused, "I wonder if my Uncle Solomon was really doing me a kindness when he left me all that money in his will."

"It's the only good thing he ever did for any of his family," Lady Arnfield observed. "Spending so much time abroad, exploring. Nasty, dirty, dangerous occupation. Still, he collected all those lovely gold treasures that made him so rich. And all the better for you."

Cliona sighed. "I almost feel that he left me too much. I have more money than anyone needs."

"Nonsense, my dear, a woman can never have too much money," asserted Lady Arnfield decisively.

"Do you think so?" Cliona murmured, half to herself. "I'm not so sure."

"Well obviously your experiences have been unlucky, but not every man is a fortune hunter. You must have met a few that you liked. Wasn't there anyone who touched your own feelings – just a little?"

Cliona nodded. "Just a little," she said impishly. "Just long enough to flirt the evening away and then forget about him."

"So you're not – in love?"

"Not the slightest. Isn't it sad? You'd think I would have fallen victim by now, but no. Sometimes I feel that I am waiting for something."

"Waiting for what?"

"I'm not sure. Just 'something'. 'Something special'.

That's all I know."

Cliona ceased her restless wanderings about the room and came to rest at the window that looked out over the surrounding countryside.

"Aunt Martha, what is that?"

"Where, my dear?"

"Beyond the trees. It looks like a fairy castle, all towers and turrets, riding against the clouds."

"Yes, it is beautiful isn't it? That's Hartley Castle, home of the Earl of Hartley. He and your uncle are great friends and great rivals too, because the Earl is the only man in the county with a better stable than ours."

Cliona, a notable horsewoman, clapped her hands in delight.

"I can't wait to meet him."

"So you shall, soon. But for now it's almost time to dress for dinner. Your uncle will be home at any moment. He would have been here to meet you, but he had an important meeting to attend. As Lord Lieutenant he has many duties."

"Of course. I'm looking forward to meeting Uncle Kenton again. Now, what shall I wear for dinner?"

The two ladies passed a pleasurable half hour, finally settling on a gown of blue satin and gauze, which set off Cliona's eyes admirably.

Then Lady Arnfield retired to her own room while Cliona's maid Sarah began to carry up water for her bath. It was bliss to wash off the dust of the journey. Afterwards she donned her gown and settled down for Sarah to dress her hair.

When she had finished there was no sign of Lady Arnfield so, being an independent girl, Cliona slipped out into the corridor and down the great stairs into the drawing room. A pair of French windows stood open, and beyond them was a large, well tended garden, full of flowers and shrubs.

But what really drew Cliona's delighted attention was the sight of a small, mischievous spaniel, with a ball that he had dropped onto the lawn, gazing at her hopefully.

"You darling!" she exclaimed. "Of course I'll come and play."

The next moment she was out of the window and skimming down the three steps onto the lawn, seizing the ball and throwing it into the distance. The spaniel barked his pleasure and began to chase it, with Cliona following, laughing.

CHAPTER TWO

Hartley Castle had been in the possession of the Hartley family for six hundred years. Starting as mere Barons, they had risen to Viscounts and then to Earls.

During all that time they had increased their wealth due to their friendship with whichever Monarch happened to be on the throne.

The castle had been added to, made less draughty and more comfortable and luxurious. An apartment was always set aside for visiting Royalty, and only two years ago the Prince of Wales had honoured them with his presence.

Charles's mother lived in an apartment in the east wing and his way to it took him along the great picture gallery, where hung pictures of almost all the family, going back for twelve generations.

Here he paused for a moment to regard some of the portraits, for his cousin's remarks about family history had made memories become alive again.

Here was his grandfather, the ninth Earl, when he had just succeeded to the title. There he was again, a year later, with his new bride. Next was the ninth Countess, holding her newly born twin sons, Simon and Arthur.

There were several portraits of the sons themselves, for they had been identical and so splendid looking that their portraits had been painted many times. Simon and Arthur at five, with matching angelic faces, at ten, still beautiful, but now Arthur was developing a scowl that all the painter's tact could not disguise.

By that time Arthur had heard the story of the swapped babies and seized on it, convinced that he, and not his brother, was the true heir. The family had dismissed it as childish fantasy, persuading themselves that he would grow out of it. But he never did.

The brothers had married in the same year and their sons, Charles and John had been born within a few months of each other.

Since they both resembled their fathers, it followed that they too looked like twins and the double portraits started again. Charles and John, childish and charming at six – Charles and John on horseback. They had been close friends then, before John had become infected by his father's obsession.

And then Simon had died unexpectedly from pneumonia, leaving a grieving widow and a sixteen year old son, Charles, now heir to the Earldom.

Charles could still clearly remember the day of his father's funeral when he had stood by the grave, fighting back tears, his mother's hand tucked into his arm. Beside him stood his grandfather, sternly repressing grief at the death of his son.

On the other side of the grave stood Arthur, in black from head to foot as befitted a man who had just lost his twin brother. Charles had looked into his face, so heartbreakingly like the dead man's. Perhaps he was seeking comfort in that resemblance. If so, he found none.

His uncle had stared back at him with a savage hostility so powerful that the grief stricken boy had instinctively turned away.

Then his eyes had sought John, whom he still thought

of as a friend.

Never more.

John's face showed the same terrible anger as his father's. It was like watching one face.

Charles had known in that moment that he had lost his friend.

His grandfather had lived another five years, dying the week after Charles's twenty-first birthday. Now Charles was the tenth Earl of Hartley, lord of all the lands around, landlord of a dozen villages and farms, squire, friend and father to 'his' people.

It was a heavy burden for a very young man, made heavier by the bitter resentment of his Uncle Arthur and cousin John. His accession had opened up old wounds.

Those wounds had never healed. And now Charles realised that they never would.

He found his mother in her sitting room accompanied by his grandmother, the widowed ninth Countess, and Jezebel, a large long-haired cat of repellent aspect, who disliked Charles as much as he disliked her.

Just why his mother, a lady of unquestioned virtue, should have chosen to name her pet after a biblical harlot was something he had never understood.

"Bless you, my dear," his mother said, greeting him with a kiss. "We saw John galloping off down the drive, and we hoped you would come to tell us all about it."

"I imagine you could guess most of it," replied Charles, kissing his grandmother, and seating his long legged figure on the sofa beside her. "He presented me with another wad of bills which he expects me to pay and I refused."

"Perfectly right," his mother said in her high voice, which had a slight hoot. "He's a bad boy. You should not give in to him. You've been much too indulgent."

17

Charles suppressed the despair that this pronouncement induced in him. His grandmother was old and increasingly out of touch with reality. She seemed to regard John as no worse than an ill-behaved youngster who could be admonished. The truth, that he was heartless, cruel and selfish, seemed to have passed her by.

Charles tried hard to protect her, but her lack of understanding increased his sense of isolation.

"I'm afraid John makes it hard not to be indulgent," he said, speaking mildly. "He spends the money first and tosses the bills to me. He knows I'll pay rather than let him go to prison and besmirch the family name."

"Heavens what a thought!" exclaimed his mother.

Before her marriage she had been Lady Hester Coledale, seventh daughter of an impoverished Earl with too many daughters and only one son.

With only a tiny fortune, she was considered lucky to have secured an Earl's heir as her husband. She became Lady Hester Baxter and the future Countess of Hartley. All seemed set fair.

But she never became a Countess. The death of her husband while his father was still alive had blighted her hopes and now her life was centred on her son.

In middle age she was still slender and elegant with the remains of girlish prettiness and a giddy, inconsequential way of talking that often masked a disconcerting sharpness of mind.

"I often think John's quite mad," she said now, working at her embroidery. "His mind is fixed on one issue and nothing else makes the slightest impression."

"Yes, maybe he is a little mad," Charles mused. "He considers himself wronged."

"Stuff and nonsense!" asserted Lady Hester robustly.

The other two looked at her.

"Stuff and nonsense!" she repeated. "Piffle and balderdash. He believes it because he wants to, just as his father did."

"I suppose there couldn't possibly be any truth in that old story of the confused midwife, mama?" Charles asked curiously.

"Confused? You mean drunk, don't you?"

"Well – I was being delicate."

"Don't be. It's an annoying habit. Say what you mean."

"I beg your pardon," he said meekly. "But could it be true?"

"Of course not," his mother replied, "for the very good reason that it's impossible. Mrs. Kenning, the midwife, could not have confused the babies, because she was never with them both together.

"She was perfectly sober when she arrived, or your grandfather would have thrown her out. She helped with Simon's birth, but then the nanny took him away. Mrs. Kenning stayed with the family, waiting for the second baby.

"While the nanny was showing Simon off to his father in another room, Arthur was born and a nursery maid took charge of him. Mrs. Kenning was paid handsomely, went out to *The Dancing Footman* and spent every penny on gin. That's where the story originated, mark my words."

His grandmother now joined in the conservation and sighed as she contemplated her younger son, now no longer with her.

"Poor Arthur!" she said. He was the brilliant one. Simon was sound and steady, but Arthur was dazzling. He could ride better and learn better, so of course he began to think he *was* better. He felt that fate had cheated him. From there it was a short step to deciding that Mrs. Kenning had cheated him."

"Perhaps in a way he had been cheated, if he really was the brilliant one," Charles mused.

"Not at all!" she stressed decidedly. "Brilliance is quite out of place in the English aristocracy. Fortunately you show no sign of it."

"Thank you, Grandmama," Charles said, his eyes dancing with appreciation.

"However, I have to say that you could have dealt with John more cleverly. It's time you thought of something. I don't want to be thrown out into the streets at my time of life."

"No, no, it's not as bad as that," Charles hastened to assure her, adding under his breath, "Not yet, at any rate."

*

Sir Kenton Arnfield reached home late that afternoon to be met by his butler with the news that Lady Cliona had arrived, and both ladies were now in their rooms dressing for dinner.

"Splendid!" he said with hearty pleasure as the butler took his coat and retired. "Ah, my dear!"

His wife was hurriedly descending the stairs, taking his arm and urging him into the drawing room.

"Quick, Cliona will be down in a moment," she said. "And I want to talk to you first."

"Is something wrong."

"Not at all. Everything is going wonderfully well. She's so sweet and unspoilt. And so beautiful. Such a season she's had, so many offers of marriage, but she's refused them all."

Sir Kenton's bluff, good natured face showed bewilderment. "Hang it, Martha! I've only just arrived home. I want my dinner. Can't we discuss Cliona's prospects later?"

"Yes of course we will. But I wanted you to understand the position before you see her. She isn't engaged, and she isn't in love with anyone." Lady Arnfield finished with an air of triumph.

Sir Kenton's wits were sound but not sharp and this pronouncement left him floundering.

"Am I expected to do something about this now?" he wanted to know. "Before dinner?"

"Oh, don't be so provoking. You know exactly what I mean."

"Yes, I'm beginning to have a worrying feeling that I do."

"She saw the turrets of Hartley Castle through her window, asked about them and seemed so interested – "

"Martha, admit the truth. You're planning to throw her into Charles's path, aren't you?"

"Not at all," Lady Arnfield said haughtily. Then her proud manner collapsed and she giggled. "Well, it won't hurt for them to meet. He's such a good looking young man, and so delightful. And an Earl. Think of it, my dear! And she will be the Countess of Hartley of Hartley Castle."

"*Will* be?" echoed her alarmed spouse. "*Might* be!"

"Oh, will be, might be! What does it matter?"

"A great deal if she turns him down as she has all the others."

"Nonsense, why should she?" she replied. "I'm sure he is the handsomest young man for miles around. Almost as handsome as you were, my love, when you were his age."

Sir Kenton accepted this flattery with a grin that revealed a great deal of husbandly cynicism.

"My dear," he said, "please don't let your ambitions run away with your common sense."

"I have no common sense," Lady Arnfield said stoutly.

"You're always saying so."

"But it is entirely unnecessary for you to prove me right. I'm not at all sure that this marriage would be a good thing. There are some very ugly rumours – "

"Oh pooh, take no notice! Lord Hartley is a good friend. You and he enjoy your rivalry about your horses."

"But this is quite different, my dear. I like Charles personally, but I would think twice about seeing Cliona married to him. If only half of what I've heard is true – of course the family does its best to keep the whole thing quiet, but talk gets out."

He sighed. "It's not Charles's fault, of course. We can't choose our relations, and he's been dashed unlucky. But there it is. Any uncle who cared for a girl's welfare would be concerned at the prospect of such a marriage."

"But Charles is such a splendid young man."

"I will agree to that. I will allow him to be all a man should be, well born, courteous, of a good character – "

"And good looks!"

"If you must, although personally I would not have rated his looks as of major importance."

Lady Arnfield sniffed. "Much you know."

"Very well, good looks, distinguished manners, and from a family that has played a noble part in our country's history. *But –* "

They exchanged significant glances.

"*But –* " his wife agreed reluctantly and sighed. "Yet don't you think Cliona might be just the girl he needs to solve his biggest problem?"

"Martha, that's enough, if you mean what I think you do. Do you expect me to help my friend at the expense of my niece? What man of honour could do so?"

"Of course you couldn't. But she must meet him, surely?"

"Of course she must. We're probably worrying about nothing. I dare say she won't take to him at all."

They moved out of the drawing room into the hall.

A moment later Cliona came slowly through the French windows. She did not make a habit of eavesdropping, but no young lady, however well brought up, could have resisted what she had just heard.

As she walked upstairs there was a mischievous smile on her lips.

*

It was a relief to Charles that his grandmother always breakfasted in her room, so that he and his mother could eat alone. It meant he could speak about his cousin more frankly. The Dowager Countess might berate John behind his back, but he was still her grandson and Charles was too kind to wound her feelings.

The morning after the quarrel, his mother joined him in the breakfast room overlooking the garden.

"You're dressed for riding, dearest. I'm glad. It will blow the cobwebs away."

"That's what I hope."

"And I suppose you're going alone?" she asked in accents of disapproval.

"Certainly I am."

Charles knew that both his father and grandfather had always ridden with one or two grooms bringing up the rear. They had felt it was part of the dignity of the family to present a sufficiently imposing appearance. But even when Charles was quite young he had always preferred to ride alone.

"But why?" his mother asked him, not for the first time. "It's so much nicer with someone to talk to."

"I don't like to talk, I prefer to think. As I grow older, I have more and more to think about than I have ever had before."

"How true," Lady Hester agreed. "But I would like you to have someone with whom you can share your troubles. Dearest boy, I am still waiting anxiously to hear of your wedding."

"There is no reason to hurry, Mama. Of course, I do realise that one day I'll have to produce a son to carry on the line."

"Well yes, there's family duty, and a son you certainly must have. But don't be so absurd as to have two at once. Really, that was a most ill-managed business. I don't know how your grandmother came to do anything so foolish."

This made him laugh. "It wasn't her fault, Mama. I don't suppose she intended it."

"Well it was very silly anyway," Lady Hester said vaguely. "But I didn't mean that. I meant that I would like to see you riding with some beautiful young woman, to whom you can give your heart."

Charles grimaced. "You ask too much, Mama. I have people worrying me all day for this and that and now you want to add another care."

"Then think of this. If anything happens to you, John will inherit the title and estate."

Charles groaned. "I know it only too well."

"Then do something about it," his mother urged him severely. "Marry, have a son, cut him out."

"And have to endure even more of his tantrums when he sees his last hope vanish? No, I thank you."

Lady Hester sighed. "As you wish, my dear boy. I

only hoped that you might give your old mother a grandson before she was too old to enjoy him. But I don't want to be unreasonable."

"Mama!" he protested, half laughing. "Stop talking like that. It's all fudge and you know it. Why you've only just passed your fiftieth birthday."

"How *dare* you!" she exclaimed in outrage. "I have *not yet* reached my fiftieth birthday."

"Strange, I thought you had. I'm thirty-two and – "

"I was a mere child when I married your father. Everyone said I looked pathetically young at our wedding."

Charles grinned. Teasing was one of his pleasures in life. And in her life too, if the truth be told.

"Very well, forty-nine," he conceded. "So no more talking as though you were in your dotage. I have a little time yet to present you with a grandchild. I want to fall in love first."

She regarded him with sympathy. "My poor boy! Have you never been in love?"

He grinned. "Yes. Far too often."

"Oh, I see. You mean something horrid."

"No, of course not. I mean something very pleasant," he said wickedly. "But not something that would lead to a Hartley heir."

"Good heavens, your father would faint if he could hear you say that. He was so rigidly virtuous. It was quite oppressive sometimes, and I really don't feel I can be blamed if – " she saw her son regarding her quizzically and added hastily, "well, never mind that."

"Too late, Mama! I've always known what a terrible flirt you were."

"Well, one has to do something to pass the time," she said, exasperated.

25

"Too true. I've found the same myself. But marriage is different. I want to marry a girl who is unique and quite different from the ordinary girls whom, to tell the truth, I find rather dull."

His mother sighed.

"Oh, how like you! You've always been very particular, darling. Or do I mean perverse? Yes, I think I do. Forever wanting something different from what you have. It's been the same since you were a baby."

"Yes, it has," he agreed, much struck. For all her feather-headed ways, Lady Hester had a habit of hitting on a truth that had occurred to nobody else. "Now I remember I was a difficult child, wanting something until Nanny had produced it, and then wanting the opposite."

He stopped suddenly, disturbed by the recollection that Nanny was one of the pensioners who depended on him now. He was still very fond of her, and often called on her in the little cottage on the estate where she lived in retirement.

He forced himself to speak brightly again.

"I think I had the idea that if I was perverse for long enough I would find perfection."

His mother nodded. But in the next moment she shook her head. "If you're looking for perfection in your wife, it's impossible, and you'll have to settle for much less."

Charles set his chin in a stubborn manner that she recognised and sighed.

"Even you won't find the perfect woman by being mulish about it," she scolded.

"Will I find her anyway? Perhaps I'm condemned to be an old bachelor."

She gave a little scream. "Not that. Think of your duty. Besides, why shouldn't you find a nice girl who will love you? I remember when you were very young the girls

26

were running after you. And you enjoyed being admired. Don't deny it."

"I don't deny it," he replied.

"There were quite a few pretty girls I remember you dancing with and spending quite a lot of time with. I quite expected you to marry one of them."

"You were arranging my marriage as far back as that?"

"These things have to be planned ahead. And when you were at Oxford you were a terrible flirt – "

"I get that from my mother," he said wickedly.

She ignored this with dignity. "I did have hopes of several of them, but they all came to nothing."

Charles gave a rueful smile.

"I suppose now I look back, I was somehow disillusioned or disappointed. As you said – too particular."

"Too intent on enjoying the bachelor life."

"That too," he admitted shamelessly.

"But now the time has come to think of the future. With John behaving like this, there's simply only one answer. You will have to marry money."

There was a shocked silence and then Charles rose violently and began to stride about the room.

"Money! Money! Money!" he said contemptuously. "Does anyone ever want anything else?"

"It happens to be exactly what you want," his mother replied.

"No, it's what I need. What I *want* is love," he answered sharply. "The love I read about in books which as far as I can find out is only found in books and not in reality."

"This sort of talk is all very fine," his mother said crossly, "but you have to marry money. John isn't going to stop, and unless you crush him he will always be there asking for more, more, more, until you don't have a penny left."

Charles stopped pacing and resumed his seat. His face was very pale.

"You're right, of course," he admitted. "Hard and miserable though it is, it's the truth. But how do you suggest I 'crush' him?"

Lady Hester sighed. "It's a problem, isn't it? Oh, how I wish this was the eighteenth century, when it was easier to have people assassinated."

Charles choked slightly into his coffee.

"Mama please, I beg you not to say things like that. I know you're only joking – "

"Am I? Well, yes I suppose I am. But sometimes I feel quite murderous towards him for his wicked selfishness. And then I cheer myself up by thinking of him being set upon by footpads and cudgelled to death. It makes me feel so much better."

Her sweet smile and her blue eyes were angelic as she spoke.

Charles had always suspected that beneath her fairy-tale fragility his mother was a much more robust character than anyone suspected. Now he regarded her cautiously, not quite knowing how to take her last remarks. She smiled and patted his hand.

"I say things I don't mean. Sometimes it helps. But then the problem is still there."

He nodded and rose to his feet, longing for the ride that would briefly set his troubles aside.

She came with him as far as the front door. Suddenly he said,

"Pray for me, Mama, that I will find the right way to handle this. Don't worry yourself, there must be a way out.

Somehow, by some miracle, I have to find it."

There were tears in his mother's eyes as she kissed him goodbye.

He headed eagerly for the stables, where the head groom was waiting for him. Charles managed to smile at the man who was a good, faithful worker.

"Lightning's been waiting for you, my Lord. Getting impatient."

"What he wants is a good gallop to take some of the energy out of him," he replied. "Well, I intend to give him the fastest gallop he's ever had."

He mounted Lightning, a gleaming black stallion and his favourite. As though tired of waiting, the animal began moving at once, out of the stable and into the paddock. As Charles tightened his reins, he had difficulty in preventing Lightning from living up to his name. The horse wanted to be given his head, but it was not until they were well into the fields which lay beyond the garden that he could have it.

For a while he galloped as fast as his legs would let him, with Charles controlling him as lightly as possible. They knew and trusted each other.

At last Lightning found it easier to settle down to a slower place. Having taken the field at an almost breathless speed, they reached the big wood. Now the horse slowed again to take the path through the trees.

For a moment Charles forgot his own troubles. The sun coming through the trees made the wood as beautiful and as mystical as he had always found it. Ever since he had been a small boy and believed there were wizards and goblins in the wood, he had always found that to ride there gave him a strange happiness which he never found anywhere else.

Even today, he never came here without half expecting some magical apparition.

'You're a fool,' he told himself. 'There's no such thing as magic. There are no spells, and no fairies.'

And then, just ahead of him, he saw a young woman.

CHAPTER THREE

For a moment Charles stared, unable to believe what he was seeing. He closed his eyes, shook his head, and then opened them again.

The apparition had vanished.

'Am I going mad?' he asked himself.

All around him the air of the woods seemed to be singing, as if to tell him that something special was happening.

Then he saw her again, riding a white horse. As he watched she disappeared between the trees, but then emerged again, straight into a shaft of sunlight that seemed to be slanting down on her directly from Heaven.

Was she real?

And if so, how had she come to be in his wood, when the entire neighbourhood knew that it was forbidden territory? Nobody was allowed here without his express permission.

'Perhaps she's a visitor in these parts,' he thought, 'and doesn't know my rules. I must tell her to go.'

But he lingered for a moment to admire the horse she was riding, as fine an animal as he had ever seen.

The young woman, too, provoked his admiration. She was young and pretty and as she moved in and out of the sunbeams, he saw the gleam of gold in her hair.

She rode out of sight and he felt a sudden fear that she would leave before he could discover who she was. He urged Lightning forward, reaching her just as she stopped by the river. Swiftly dismounting, she tied her horse's reins to a tree and bent down to admire the kingcups, which made a golden picture.

'As golden as herself,' he thought involuntarily.

She seemed unaware of him as he rode nearer, absorbed in the beauty of the flowers and the water. He thought he had never witnessed a more delightful scene.

Then suddenly she became aware of his presence and raised her head. He saw that she was not only very pretty, but undoubtedly a lady, dressed in an exquisite grey riding habit. As she rose to her feet, he could see that the habit looked as if it had been tailored especially for her elegant figure.

"Good morning," Charles ventured. "I am afraid you are trespassing."

"Oh dear, am I?" she asked. "I'm a stranger here."

"I thought you must be."

He dismounted and came closer. Now he could see that her eyes were the blue of the sky.

"I'm so sorry," she said, "but the gate was open and the river was shining in the sun, so I was curious."

Charles smiled.

"I can understand that," he said. "I also find the river is very beautiful where one least expects it."

She chuckled, and to his enchanted ear it was like the rippling of the water.

"That's just how it should be," she said. "Beautiful where one least expects it. Don't you think the unexpected is always nicer?"

"Not always," he said, "but sometimes, yes."

At that moment he felt very strongly that the unexpected was charming. What could be more unexpected than this vision? And what could be more charming?

He wondered why, if she was staying in the neighbourhood, he had not been invited to meet her. It was an unwritten law that if he, the Lord Lieutenant, or any other of the local gentry, had someone new or exciting visiting them, their nearest neighbours were automatically asked to dine and be introduced.

"Well, I suppose I should be going," said the vision.

"So soon?" he protested. "When we have only just met?"

A moment ago he had been planning to order her off, but now nothing was further from his intentions.

"Well, you say I am trespassing," she explained. "So perhaps I should hurry away before the owner finds me and has me arrested."

"He would have to be very hard-hearted to do that," said Charles.

"Really? Do you know him?"

"Very well."

She regarded him with her head on one side. "I've heard that he's a terrible man. Harsh and cruel?"

"Positively wicked," he confirmed, his eyes dancing.

"Nobody dares cross him."

"They regret it if they do," Charles agreed.

"I think I had better go."

"And I think I had better introduce myself," said Charles, "before my character is completely ruined. Lord Hartley ma'am, at your service."

She chuckled. "Now why didn't it occur to me that's who you might be."

She offered him her hand and he enclosed it between both of his, laughing with her. It was like holding the hand of a fairy, he thought, a being from another world, sent to enchant him.

"I am Lady Cliona Locksley," she said.

"Then your father was – ?"

"Lord Locksley. He died last year, and my mother the year before. Mama was the sister of Lady Arnfield and she and Sir Kenton invited me to stay with them."

"Ah yes, I seem to recall him mentioning a niece who was to visit them soon," said Charles, frowning.

"I wonder how he referred to me," said Cliona impishly. "He didn't by any chance call me 'that wretched girl'?"

"No, I'm sure he didn't."

"But you can't be certain?"

In fact Charles's memory was vague because these days his troubles dominated his thoughts, so that sometimes he hardly heard what was said to him.

"Quite certain," he said firmly. To change the difficult subject, he said,

"How do your aunt and uncle feel about you riding about the countryside alone, without a groom to assist you?"

"Well," she said in the manner of one making a confession, "they don't really know."

"Don't *really* know?" he queried.

"They don't know at all," she confessed. "But when Uncle Kenton said that Pagan was mine to ride while I was here – well – I had to try him out."

"Of course, but without a groom?"

"I did mean to take a groom. He got Pagan ready for me and helped me to mount, and then someone called him. He said, 'Just a minute, miss,' and – " she shrugged with a smile as mischievous as a little girl who knew she had to be forgiven.

"When the poor fellow came back, you'd gone," Charles finished.

"Yes, I suppose I had."

"And what will happen to him?"

"Nothing, because I shall tell Uncle Kenton that he wasn't to blame."

"What happens when you want to remount?"

She gave him a sideways look. It occurred to Charles that all her life this charming creature had had people rushing to please her. Yet strangely it hadn't spoilt her.

"Let me assist you," he said.

After he had thrown her lightly up into the saddle and mounted Lightning, they began to walk their horses through the trees.

"So you are Lord Hartley," she said. "They were talking about you at dinner last night, about all the things you've done for the county. They are obviously very proud of you."

"I am delighted to hear such flattering remarks straight from the horse's mouth, so to speak," said Charles.

"You mean straight from the mare's mouth, don't you?" she teased.

"I should never be so impolite, ma'am, as to call you a mare," he said, rallying his wits.

"But then you've called me a horse," she pointed out.

He was silent, looking at her imploringly. He was not used to young women who engaged him in a duel of wits, and left him with the alarming impression that he was coming off worse.

Seeing his confusion she relented. "I'm sorry for trespassing," she said. "But with your land being next to

35

Uncle Kenton's, I'm afraid I was tempted."

"You are very welcome and I hope you'll come again."

"I was not welcome when you first saw me. You scowled terribly."

"My mind was on other things," he said hastily. "I'm afraid I can be a bit of a bear sometimes."

"I don't believe that," she said sweetly.

And suddenly, he did not believe it either.

"I really do hope you will come back to my land, and ride wherever you please," he said.

"How lovely. I've never been to this part of England before and I find it fascinating."

"Then let me show you some more of it. If you'd like to ride a little further on, you will see the best place to bathe. I've always enjoyed swimming there. Not only is it warm, as it is at the moment, but I have the whole place to myself."

"All to yourself," she echoed eagerly. "Yes, that's the best part. I've always longed to own a river of my own, where I can bathe without having a lot of people splashing about, or making it impossible for me to swim and – and – just dream."

"And what do you dream about?"

"Oh, all sorts of wonderful things. Anything that's – " she seemed to struggle for the right words, "anything that's out of this world."

Charles raised his eyebrows.

"Is that what swimming means to you?" he asked. "A chance to escape from the troubles in the world?"

She nodded her head eagerly, so that the little feather on her charming hat fluttered.

"That's exactly what I feel. But I've never met anyone else who felt the same. They all want to bounce around and make a noise, but what I want to enjoy is the ecstasy of being alone in the silver water and the golden sunshine."

It was strange, almost uncanny, to find someone who echoed his own thoughts and feelings so closely.

"I think, at heart, we all want to feel that kind of peace," he said, speaking hesitantly, for he wasn't used to sharing his innermost thoughts with others. "But unfortunately most of us have troubles. Like you, I find it easier not to think about them when I'm bathing in the river, but they are still waiting for me when I get out."

She nodded. "That's true of course. But sometimes when the sun is as bright as today and the water is clear and reflecting only the sky, we can forget the world and be in a small heaven of our own."

Charles stared at her, astonished and intrigued. He had never met a woman who had talked to him in such a way, as though the words came not from a light heart, but from a deep soul.

Of course, she might have been playing a part, something he suspected a lot of women did very easily, in order to confuse and baffle men. But he did not think so. He was quite certain that she was speaking the truth from the very depths of her being.

While they talked they had moved slowly along the side of the river. Now, just ahead of them, was the place where Charles had bathed. There were tall trees on both sides of the river, which meandered away, deeper into the wood, and kingcups flowering right down to the water's edge.

"It is lovely, so lovely!" Cliona exclaimed. "How can it be so marvellous and not have hoards of people trespassing?"

"They are too kind to me or too afraid of me," Charles replied with a smile. "It is known as a special part of my grounds and I am proud to say I have very few trespassers."

"Like me," she said shyly. "I am sorry but they didn't tell me that you do not allow people on your land. As the gate was open and it looked so entrancing, I just came in."

"I should have been there to welcome you," he said. "Now we've met I can only hope you will come again. Perhaps I'll find you here tomorrow morning,"

"Is this the time you always ride?" Cliona asked.

"When I'm at home and of course when I have things to think about," Charles replied. "I find nothing more peaceful or more helpful than this particular part of the river."

"But you like to be alone here," she said suddenly. "I'm right, aren't I? This is your special place for being alone."

He took some time to answer, because he had the feeling that it was vital to get his answer right. She was too important for meaningless words.

"Everyone has times when they want to be alone – usually when you can't find an answer to a very difficult question," he said at last.

Hearing his grave tone, Cliona knew that the problems that had brought him to the river this morning were not light ones.

"How can you be troubled in such a beautiful place?" she asked. "When they were talking about you at dinner last night, I was almost sure you were different from everyone else and you were almost supreme."

"If, by supreme, you mean able to rise above the world's cares," he answered, "then no man is supreme in that sense. No matter how fortunate or happy we might seem, there are always snares in the undergrowth, waiting to pull us down, often when we least expect it."

She looked at him with sympathy, but stayed silent, waiting for him to continue. After a while he said,

38

"We may hide our problems, but they stay with us until we find a way to solve them – if there *is* a way."

He added the last words without meaning to. He had not intended to reveal his own suffering, but against his will it was there in his voice.

"The beauty of this place is only part of my world," he added. "I cannot live here always. If only I could. Here I can escape, but only briefly."

"I am so sorry," she said gently. "It is easy for me to talk, but it isn't easy for you, is it?"

"Sometimes there seems to be no sunshine at all," he said heavily.

He wondered what had come over him to be having such a conversation with a stranger. Particularly a young girl whom he had only just met. He tried to pull himself together and change the subject.

But before he could do so, she said quietly,

"I will pray that whatever is wrong and upsetting you is drowned by this golden, glittering river, and that you find the real happiness and love you are seeking."

The words came very softly and gently from her lips. It was as though she could look into his heart and read every despairing thought.

Charles stared at her in surprise. Then he said,

"Thank you. I only hope that what you have wished for me will happen."

"I will pray for it," she repeated fervently.

Gradually the trees were thinning and the river was leading them out into the fields.

Then, speaking lightly, as if she felt they had been too serious, she said,

"I'll race you to the other end of the field and see if my horse is better than yours."

Without waiting for a reply she started off riding swiftly. Watching her he saw that she was an excellent rider. Her horse was larger than most women would have chosen, but she handled him with easy confidence.

He did not have to tell Lightning that this was a race. As long as Charles had owned him he had never yet lost a race or failed to pass any other horse who challenged him. Now he broke into a gallop.

Soon they were going at a speed that left no doubt that this was a genuine race. And for once, he could not be certain of winning.

'How many women could ride like this?' he wondered in admiration.

On and on they galloped.

The end of the field was in sight. The two horses needed no encouragement to strive against each other. Only the appearance of a hedge forced them to a standstill.

A dead heat.

"That was wonderful!" she cried ecstatically. "I've never ridden so fast and your horse is magnificent."

"I think you are an excellent rider," Charles told her. "Neither of us can claim to be the winner."

"No, that's the wrong way to look at it," she assured him.

"What should I have said?"

"We can both claim victory. That's much better."

"Yes, it is," he said at once. "When I came out this morning, I was feeling very depressed. But you have cheered me up. Now I know that nobody has the right to be unhappy or worried in these beautiful surroundings."

She nodded and he felt she understood him. The torment in his mind and the despair in his heart were clear to her without any further explanation.

And yet she was so young, not yet twenty, he guessed. He had never found young girls very interesting to talk to. They had not lived very long, and so understood little.

Now here was this unusual girl teaching him that what mattered were the instincts of the heart. There was something about her that made him feel safe, as though no problem on earth could be too difficult as long as she was beside him. Yet at the same time she was thrilling and irresistible.

"I'll send an invitation to your uncle and aunt to bring you to dine at the castle," he said.

"I should love that," she said eagerly. "I can see your castle from my window and it looks so intriguing. Is it as exciting inside as outside?"

"I hope you will find it so, but I must warn you that one thing I've learned in life is that if you never expect more than is possible, you are never disappointed."

But she shook her head eagerly. "No, I'm sure that's wrong. You should always hope to find something unique, something you've never found before. Which means that you don't have any expectations. That can be the best way."

Charles laughed. "That is one way of looking at it," he admitted. "I only hope you won't be disappointed with my house, my dinner or me."

She laughed. "You are asking a great deal," she teased. "At the same time if I were to have a bet, I feel sure I wouldn't lose it."

"That is a compliment," he answered with a smile. "I shall show you over the castle myself and I await your opinion with trepidation."

As they talked the Lord Lieutenant's house came into view and already they could see figures in the yard, regarding them with anxious interest. Cliona waved to them cheekily.

41

"I'll leave you now to make your explanations," Charles said wryly.

"And you will go back to your problems," she said. "But please don't worry. You will find the answer."

"The answer?"

"To the terrible question that is tormenting you."

He stared at her. "But – "

"You think there is no answer, don't you? But there is. Believe me, there is."

"How on earth can you know?"

"I feel it," Cliona replied. "I sometimes feel these things and nine times out of ten what I have felt is true."

"What are you?" he asked abruptly. "A witch?"

"Well, if I am, I'm not a bad witch. Truly."

"I believe you," he said, speaking as if in a dream. "I can't begin to imagine where you get your mysterious powers, but I believe they are good and kind."

For a moment he was desperately tempted to tell her everything, to lay his woes before her and seek help from her generous spirit. But she was young and innocent and for all her wisdom, she could know little of the world. Such help was not for him.

"If my 'mysterious powers' can have any effect at all," she said earnestly, "I will exert them all for you. And I pray that you may find the sunshine again. In fact, I am certain of it."

She did not wait for him to reply, but spurred her horse on in the direction of the house.

The Earl watched her go, thinking it had been one of the most extraordinary and unusual conversations he had ever had with anyone, least of all a young lady.

'She is unique, not like anyone else I have ever known,' he said to himself as he turned Lightning for home.

All the way back to the castle he was brooding about Cliona. He rode into the stable yard, dismounted and let his groom take the horse and while he threw the man a pleasant word his thoughts were elsewhere.

'Only an hour ago I didn't even know she existed,' he thought as he went into the hall. 'Yet now I know that she is going to change my life – no, she *has* changed it. I can never be the same again.'

Then he stood still as a stunning thought occurred to him.

'And nor do I want to be the same. Not ever. For the rest of my life.'

It was like the sun coming out, a glorious radiance flooding him as though Cliona had left her gift of sunshine with him.

He began to run and did not stop until he reached his mother's apartment.

"Mama, how quickly can you arrange a dinner party?" he asked. "Tomorrow?"

"If absolutely necessary. It depends how important it is. Who will be coming?"

"The Arnfields and their visitor, a niece of Lady Arnfield I believe."

Conscious of his mother's shrewd eyes on him, he added casually, "I would not wish to be backward in my attention to our neighbours."

"Is she pretty?" Lady Hester asked.

"Really Mama, I haven't said I've met her – "

"I know, but is she pretty."

Charles gave a shrug which he meant to seem devil-may-care, but which to his mother seemed steeped in guilt.

"Passable, I suppose," he said casually.

'She's more than pretty,' she thought.

Aloud she said, "Does she have any money?"

"I didn't ask her," Charles said, aghast. "Has it come to this? Must that be the first question in everyone's mind?"

"Yes, it has come to this and you know very well why, so let us not deceive ourselves. Does she have any money?"

"I would imagine her to be reasonably prosperous but not a great heiress. At least, I hope she isn't a great heiress, since I couldn't – that is, I imagine there's little fear of that. The Arnfields are not enormously wealthy and Lord Locksley had a reputation as a very heavy gambler. I doubt there was much left when he died."

"Then you cannot afford to marry her."

"I wasn't even thinking of – " He checked himself. There was no deceiving his mother.

"Just arrange the dinner party please, Mama. I want everything to be of the very best and the invitations should go out as soon as possible."

He left the room quickly before she could ask any more questions.

*

"Cliona, my dear girl, it was very naughty of you to gallop off alone like that."

Lady Arnfield had shooed the maid out of Cliona's bedroom, so that she might help her niece take off her riding habit and enjoy a comfortable gossip at the same time.

"I know, dear Aunt Martha and I'm sorry. You will make sure Uncle Kenton knows it wasn't Harris's fault, won't you?"

"I promise you Harris won't get into any trouble. I shall blame it all on you. Will that satisfy you? Cliona?"

"I'm sorry, Aunt," she said, giving herself a little shake.

"You were in another world, my dear. What has made

you so thoughtful?"

"Oh nothing, it's just – have you ever plunged into something thinking it was going to be a delightful joke, and then discovered that it wasn't funny at all? In fact it was terribly sad and serious and all you wanted to do was to make it right."

Cliona saw her aunt's baffled face in the mirror and recovered herself.

"Take no notice of me. I'm in a strange mood. It makes everything look different."

"A good lunch will put you to rights." She rose to depart. At the door she looked back to say,

"Don't worry about your mood. I'm sure it will pass soon."

She bustled out, leaving Cliona gazing at her reflection in the mirror, thinking how altered it looked already.

The reflection smiled back at her, with a mysterious smile, full of joy and discovery, and the secret knowledge they had shared since this morning.

'Oh no,' she murmured. 'Somehow, I don't think it will pass.'

CHAPTER FOUR

The dinner party was set, not for the following day, but the one after, and the invitations were despatched that afternoon. The acceptances came back immediately. Nobody was going to refuse the honour of dining at the castle.

"The Honourable Mr. and Mrs. Dalrymple are coming," said Lady Hester. "The vicar and his wife, also their married son and daughter who are visiting."

They were sitting in the drawing room after dinner. Tea had just been served. The Dowager Countess was assiduously working on a shapeless piece of embroidery that had occupied her for years. Lady Hester was compiling a guest list.

"Sir Kenton and Lady Arnfield, and their niece Lady Cliona," continued Lady Hester.

She paused for a reaction. Receiving none, she stole a glance at her son, but he was leaning back in his armchair, studying the painted ceiling with great attention. She glanced up, seeking in the smirking cherubs and winged warriors some hint of what made the ceiling so fascinating to her offspring. Failing to find it, she returned to her task.

"Lord and Lady Markham have accepted," she said, "and also – "

"And also your favourite nephew, whom you

neglected to invite," came a merry voice from the doorway.

Everyone looked up sharply, and Charles jumped to his feet.

"Freddy, by all that's wonderful! It's good to see you."

He strode across the room, hand outstretched to grasp the hand of a bright faced young man of about twenty. Freddy Mason was Lady Hester's nephew by one of her many sisters.

His merry spirit and sweet temper made him a family favourite. Both Lady Hester and the Countess smiled at him with pleasure, and he kissed them before accepting the glass of wine Charles poured him, and then settling himself comfortably onto the sofa.

"And to what do we owe this unexpected pleasure?" asked Charles, "surely your family home is nearby?"

"Ah, well – " Freddy began uneasily.

"The university term has finished," Charles continued remorselessly, "so even you can't have been sent down."

"No, I wasn't sent down," Freddy confirmed eagerly.

"Then you must have failed your exams," Charles finished triumphantly.

"I didn't – exactly fail – "

"But you didn't – exactly – pass either, did you?"

"I say, old fellow, I thought you'd be glad to see me – family ties and all that." Freddy said, sounding aggrieved. He sighed heavily. "But, I see how it is, a chap should know when he isn't wanted." He began to rise.

"Stop," Lady Hester ordered imperiously. "You cannot leave before the dinner party. I need another man to make up the numbers."

"You see, I am good for something," said Freddy immediately.

"Stop playing the giddy fool and come upstairs,"

Charles adjured him. "Tell your man to take your things up to your usual room – "

"Actually, old chap – "

"Of course, you've already done so. How foolish of me."

"Well, you're such a curmudgeon that I thought I'd better settle in before you could throw me out," countered Freddy innocently.

Charles clapped him on the shoulder and the two men left the room, laughing and talking.

But once they had reached Charles's room Freddy's ebullient manner became more subdued.

"I gather things are getting worse," he said.

"Now what makes you say that?" Charles asked jovially. "Look around you. Do you see anything wrong?"

"I see a number of spaces where there used to be valuable antiques," said Freddy frankly.

"I disposed of a few pieces I have no further use for." Charles tried to keep up the bright front, but it faded before Freddy's expression.

"What is it?" he asked heavily.

"I was in London last night," said Freddy, "and I went out with a few friends, just to relax after the strain of exams, you know."

"You went somewhere disreputable, I suppose."

"Just a little place where a fellow can do a bit of gambling."

Charles groaned.

"And John was there losing even more money, I suppose?"

"Well no," replied Freddy, "he happened to be on a winning streak for once. But it's very rare. I was talking to one of the stewards who sees him in there a great deal. Sometimes he does win a lot."

"I didn't know that. Not that it makes any difference since he obviously loses it all again."

"There's a cloud over his winnings too, a lot of suspicion – "

"Oh God!" Charles groaned.

"But they cannot catch him cheating, and nobody knows how he does it. I gather he haunts several of these dens so that one place doesn't get tired of him and throw him out. So, he wins a lot and loses a lot."

"And this time he was winning, so what worried you?"

"The way he was talking about you."

"Oh that," Charles sighed. "He's in a rage because I wouldn't give him any more money yesterday."

Freddy nodded. "That explains it. He was drunk and hurling abuse at you."

"What was it this time? Did I steal his inheritance?"

"Yes, he told anyone who would listen. But they'd all heard it before and weren't interested. Nobody believes it, Charles."

"But it damages the family, just the same."

Suddenly he moved over to the window and threw it open. The sun had set over the valley and lights were coming on in the houses he could see. There was the village and beyond it the farms. And there, to one side, was the home of the Lord Lieutenant, his wife and his niece.

"Look down there," he said to Freddy, who came to stand beside him. "Most of them are 'my' people. My tenants. My employees. They rely on me to look after them, keep their homes repaired, charge them reasonable rents and plough that rent back into the farms instead of bleeding them white and spending the money on myself."

"I know some landlords do that," agreed Freddy. "But you've never been one of them."

"I've prided myself on being a good landlord, but now I wonder how good. There are repairs out there that weren't done as soon as they should have been."

"Because of John?"

"Because of John. I've sold things where I felt they wouldn't be noticed, because once people start to notice the gaps – as you did – then the outside world will start to find out how bad things are. And that is something I could not bear.

"I am proud, maybe too proud for the situation I find myself in. My pride makes me try to live up to my situation, my title. It makes me wince at the thought of the outside world knowing the truth. But soon everyone will know. I keep thinking I should sell some of my race horses – "

"No," Freddy protested. "It's the big local festivity, seeing your horses win. And the world really would notice that."

"That's what I tell myself. But they'll be the next to go, unless John's winning streak continues. But it won't. How can it? What really infuriates me about John is that because of him others will suffer."

"Don't pay him any more," Freddy said violently.

"And if he goes to prison? That touches my pride too."

"Charles, you're not saving him from prison, you're just postponing it. He'll drain you of every penny and when there's none left he'll go on spending. He'll end up in a debtor's gaol and all your sacrifices will be for nothing. So why make them?"

"It's easy to say that, Freddy, but I still cling to the hope that I can save everything I love, and the people to whom I owe a duty."

He refilled Freddy's glass.

"You'll hardly credit my mother's suggestion for solving the problem," he said, trying to sound cheerful. "She wants me to marry money."

"Are you in love with any money?" Freddy asked at once.

"I believe the idea is that I should first find some money and then arrange to fall in love with it," said Charles wryly. "I suppose if I had any idea of my duty, that's what I would have to do."

Freddy gave his irrepressible grin.

"I heard you were rather good at falling in love," he said.

"What?"

"You're still a legend at Oxford."

"I didn't know that," replied Charles, startled.

"Your amatory career is spoken of in hushed tones. And there's one particular story about the Dean's wife – "

"That's enough of that," said Charles hurriedly. "It's very late and you've had a long journey."

"And you want me to go to bed?" Freddy asked. "Certainly not. This conversation is becoming very interesting."

"My 'amatory career' has been much exaggerated," said Charles vaguely.

"Don't be a spoil sport. Were you really a 'rake and a hellion'?"

Charles grinned. "Yes. But in my own defence I plead that I inherited the title much too young. No man should be an Earl at twenty-one. Too much, too soon. It ruins the character.

"I soon realised that if I pursued a young girl, or even flirted with her, her parents would get to work, attracted by the title and soon I'd be forced to offer for her.

"And she was very unlikely to refuse. I say that without conceit, because I know it wasn't myself that was the attraction."

He gave a grunt of self-mocking laughter. "I learned that the hard way. I fell madly in love and came to the verge of declaring myself. But just in time I overheard her tell a friend that I bored her to tears. It was only my title that made her give me a second glance. She was a thousand times more worldly wise than I."

"Lord, what a story!" Freddy exclaimed.

"Oh, I'm grateful to her. She taught me a lesson that I couldn't have learned any other way – not so quickly and thoroughly anyway."

"What happened after that?"

"I avoided young girls like the plague, and turned my attentions elsewhere."

"To married women. I know."

"How do you know?" asked Charles wrathfully.

"I hear the talk."

"Such talk will scorch your young ears."

Freddy grinned. "My young ears have already been scorched. It's too late to protect me now, so let's hear the rest."

Charles sighed as those days came back to him.

He had discovered that the world was full of wives who were not averse to a flirtation, or more. Often they were married to men their parents had chosen for them. They had done their duty and filled their nurseries with their husband's offspring, and now they were ready for romance with a handsome young man.

"You have to be careful not to antagonise the husbands," he told Freddy. "Choose carefully. A man who

52

enjoys long fishing trips is a good idea. If he goes abroad a lot, that's even better. Diplomats are very useful."

"Good Lord!" Freddy exclaimed suddenly. "That story about the Under Secretary in Paris, and his wife wouldn't go with him because of the children – they told him he'd been promoted to Prussia, and he hurried home to tell her, and they say her lover only just escaped out of the bedroom window in time."

Charles regarded him blandly. "I have no idea what you're talking about," he said.

"Of course you haven't."

"And if you intend to embark on a disreputable career, you'll have to be more discreet than that. No gentleman of honour ever discusses the windows he's jumped out of."

"But did you ever – ?"

"What – ?"

"After the girl you told me about, did you ever actually fall in love again?"

"Oh yes," murmured Charles. "Far too often for my own good, or theirs."

"But I mean – was it real?"

It took Charles a long time to answer.

"Yes," he said at last. "It always felt real. And yet – "

He fell silent. He was fond of Freddy, but he couldn't tell him about the sudden dissatisfaction that assailed him, a realisation that when love was 'real' too often, it had never been real at all.

He had told his mother that he sought love, speaking like a man who had never known it. And now he wondered if he had understood himself better than he had suspected.

Suddenly he couldn't bear this conversation any longer.

"That's it, young man," he said, rising quickly and

hauling Freddy to his feet. "Now you really are going to bed."

And Freddy who, beneath his light hearted ways, had a lot of insight, squeezed his shoulder and left without a word.

Left alone, Charles intended to go to bed, but instead he wandered restlessly round his room. The talk with Freddy had unsettled him, recalling the man he had been years ago and who now seemed nothing like himself.

In fact, he rather disliked that younger self. There was a selfish, calculating side to him that made a displeasing memory for a man grown older, wiser and more generous.

He had enjoyed his love affairs, which had been passionate on both sides. Despite his modest words he knew that women found him personally very attractive. He was, in many ways, an experienced and fascinating lover, as more than one high-born wife had told him.

Even now he could vividly remember the wonderful nights, the infatuation, and the hint of danger. It had been brilliant and exciting.

'Life should always be as glorious and happy as this,' he had told himself once.

That had been his guide when one romance ended and he was free to seek another.

Now he thought he must have been rather a callow young man to have expected life to be nothing but a round of pleasure. Yet he could still recall the thrill of kissing some beautiful woman for the first time.

Whether he had been flirting or in love, his heart had turned over, and he had felt a quiver of excitement which no other pleasure had given him. And he had known that the lady loved him equally.

In those days his feelings had been easily engaged. He had loved, in some cases adored the woman he was making

54

his, whose kiss had been like a touch from the stars themselves.

But he had never yet wanted any of them to run away with him, or to remain with him for the rest of his life.

He had always found that no matter how intense the bliss, it soon faded and passed.

Sooner or later, he would be seeking the same passion with another beautiful woman. And another. Because while they could satisfy his senses, they could never content his heart.

Now he knew that it was this contentment that he had always secretly sought. And if he made the dutiful marriage his family needed, then his last chance would have gone.

Well, let it go.

He told himself it would be better if he stopped making a fuss and simply bite the bullet, as other men had done before him.

And then, without warning, into his mind came the girl he had talked to that morning by the river. The beautiful girl with sunlight in her hair, who had told him gently and sweetly that she would pray for all his troubles to be over.

'Now I know I'm getting addled in the head,' he told himself with grim humour. 'She almost persuaded me that she could cast a spell that would make everything right. It's time I came down to earth.

'She is lovely, but what of that? She has no money. I can't afford to allow myself to become attracted to her.'

He tried to persuade himself to finally silence the inner voice that told him there were other more important issues.

She was gentle and innocent and for the first time it occurred to him that his own colourful past might set too great a barrier between himself and such a girl.

And in a moment of madness he had invited her to

dinner at the castle. He would have given anything to cancel it all.

He drank a large glass of whisky before going to bed. It was the only way to sleep.

*

Despite his good resolutions he found, when he mounted Lightning next morning that he instinctively turned in the direction of the wood.

There was, after all, no reason why he shouldn't ride in his own woods.

But she was not there.

To his astonishment he found himself angry. She had asked him yesterday if this was his time for riding here, which was as good as a hint that she would join him. But then she had let him down.

He drew a sharp breath, realising that his violent disappointment was a warning.

He rode on, not looking where he was going nor caring very much.

But then, from somewhere up ahead, he heard the sound of splashing and he urged Lightning forward, hardly daring to hope.

He saw her horse first. The splendid white stallion she had ridden yesterday was there, tied to a tree, nibbling contentedly at the grass.

From somewhere past the bushes the sound of splashing water became louder now. Dismounting, he tied Lightning to a post and walked forward quietly until he could part the leaves.

And there he saw a nymph, a water Goddess.

She was standing in the river, the water up to her waist, bringing first one hand then the other down on the surface, so that water shot up in sprays.

As each spray peaked in the light, it fragmented the sun into sparkling coloured droplets, so that the girl seemed to be surrounded by rainbows.

She was laughing with the blissful exuberance of a child who had forgotten the world and was totally involved with the beauty she was creating. And, watching such a creature, he too could forget the world, he realised.

He could see only the top half of her. She seemed to be wearing a bathing costume of deep blue. Probably the same blue as her eyes, he thought, wishing he was close enough to tell. It showed off her long neck and the short sleeves revealed her pretty arms.

On her head she wore a cap, decorated with daisies, which covered her hair, except for a few shining strands.

He realised that, in watching her, unseen, he was behaving in a disgraceful and ungentlemanly fashion and should leave immediately.

But suppose she got into difficulties, with nobody here to help her? No gentleman could depart and leave a girl at risk of drowning.

The fact that she herself seemed untroubled by any danger briefly sank this argument, but he remembered in time that it was for a man's superior intellect to judge these things. Women were frail and should be protected from their own rashness.

So he remained where he was, watching her with a kind of aching delight.

She stopped splashing and began to swim, making incisive strokes through the water. Charles remembered her on horseback, controlling the big animal with a strength that was belied by her slight appearance.

He could see that strength again now, and he thought that this was no frail little creature who would always have to be propped up by a man. She was a force in her own right, ready to stand by the man she had chosen and add her power to his.

Then he told himself that he had no right to think such thoughts.

She had reached a part of the river where he knew the water was deeper. There was a large rock and she hauled herself up onto it, finding a foothold and climbing to the top.

Now he could not help seeing that the rest of her shape was as beautiful as the upper part. The swimming costume flared into a little skirt, beneath which were drawers that came down almost to her knees.

She had long, graceful legs and slim ankles. Charles knew that he should avert his eyes modestly from her ankles, so he did so, looking upwards instead.

But this was no better, since she had now placed her hands behind her and thrown back her head so that the sun gleamed directly onto her throat and neck, making a long, beautiful line down to her bosom.

She was magnificent, voluptuous. Her abandoned attitude left no doubt of it. He stood transfixed, despising himself, yet fearful lest she see him and lose her charming unselfconsciousness.

But then she did something that took his breath away. Sitting forward, she brought her hands to her front and clasped them together, bending her head so that he could no longer see her face. She became very still.

It looked as though she were praying, Charles thought and knew that now he had to leave. But before he could move, she lifted her head, gazing into the sky, as though communing directly with Heaven.

She seemed to be speaking directly to a friend in whom she had total confidence, and saying,

'You have understood, haven't you? I can leave it with you?'

58

He was so sure that those words were coming from her heart that he could almost hear them.

And suddenly he knew that she was praying for himself. It was completely irrational. Why should he think she was remembering him?

But he knew that she was. This was the place where they had been together and where she had promised to pray for him.

He held his breath.

She rose to her feet, placed her hands together and dived swiftly. He had a vision of a blue mermaid flying through the air, then vanishing into the water. A moment later he saw her striking out for the bank.

He waited until she had reached it safely and was on dry land. Then he backed quietly away, retrieved his horse and departed from the wood.

He supposed that he should be ashamed of having watched her while she was unaware and in a sense he was. Not for gazing on her pretty figure, but for intruding on her prayers.

And yet, when he thought that he might be the beneficiary of those generous, innocent prayers, he knew that he would not have given up that knowledge for anything the world had to offer.

CHAPTER FIVE

Charles was in a dark mood as he dressed for dinner the following evening. How could he be pleasant to people when his misery dominated his mind to the exclusion of all else? He wanted only to be left alone.

His exhilaration at seeing Cliona the previous day had abated. The thought of her saddened him. Now that he knew himself to be cut off from her by family duty, he did not even want to see her. It seemed to him as if he was caught in some terrible trap from which there was no escape. And he was resolved not to embroil her in it.

Watkins, his butler, who had been with him a long time, sensed that he was upset. He tried to cheer him up by talking of the forthcoming horse races, at which Charles, a keen racing man, was bound to have winners.

"Especially Firefly," Watkins volunteered. "There are lots of people in the village who've been saving up so that they can go and see Firefly win, my Lord. In fact they've put a great deal of money on him."

At one time this would have delighted Charles. Now it was another reminder of how people depended on him, and how his failure could injure them.

"I hope they haven't taken too many risks," he said gloomily.

"Oh, go on with you, my Lord. You and I know there's

no one to equal him when he gets going. There now, you look splendid, just as everyone will expect."

"Yes," Charles murmured heavily. "Everyone expects."

But when it was time for his guests to arrive, he straightened his shoulders, fixed a smile on his face and walked downstairs to the drawing room, looking as though he did not have a care in the world.

From the hall below he could hear the first arrivals, the carriages halting on the gravel, the murmur of servants receiving cloaks and hats from the guests. Then footsteps climbing the stairs, Watkins entering the room announcing one couple after another.

The guests were in full evening dress, the men in white ties and the ladies in low cut evening gowns bedecked in sparkling jewels. Couple by couple they trooped in, the ladies slightly in advance of the gentlemen, as etiquette prescribed. Charles greeted them genially, while all the time his mind was listening for the carriage that would bring *her*.

"Welcome to the castle," he said a dozen times. "Delighted to see you again – yes – yes – "

At last he heard the sounds he has been waiting for. Watkins entered the drawing room and announced,

"Sir Kenton and Lady Arnfield, and Lady Cliona Locksley."

And there she was, so much more beautiful than in his imagination, a dream in pink silk and lace, pearls about her neck and in her hair. This was a new Cliona, different from the practical girl who had raced with him or the water nymph. This was a magnificent Cliona, a beauty who would attract the admiring glances of men and the envious ones of women.

As she glided towards him he heard Lady Arnfield say,

"Allow me to introduce my niece Cliona, who has just

arrived to stay with us for a while. She has heard so much about you and is longing to meet you."

Surprised by the word 'introduce' Charles raised his eyebrows at Cliona and received in return the slightest shake of the head.

So, he thought, she had not told anyone of their meeting.

He bowed gravely over her hand and their eyes met again. Hers were alight with amusement.

At his shoulder Freddy gave a significant cough.

"May I introduce my cousin, Frederick Mason?" he said.

"Sir." Cliona gave Freddy a little curtsy and he offered her a look of blatant admiration, which Charles found strangely displeasing.

More introductions, Lady Hester, the Dowager Countess. At last the entire party had assembled.

Charles drew Cliona aside.

"It never occurred to me that you hadn't told them we had already met," he said.

"I'm sorry," replied Cliona. "I should have found a way to warn you, although I'm not sure how. I was going to tell them and then – somehow I couldn't. It would have spoilt it."

He found that he understood her exactly. Those precious moments between them had been just for themselves, perfect, untouched by the world. To have let the world's curious eyes witness their secret would have been to spoil it.

When everybody was assembled Watkins declared, "dinner is served."

Freddy offered his arm to Lady Cliona.

"Allow me to escort you into dinner," he said gallantly.

"Lady Cliona is the guest of honour," said Charles firmly edging him aside. "And it is my privilege to take her in to dinner."

Freddy accepted this rebuff with good humour and promptly turned his attention to another, less sought-after damsel.

Charles bowed to Cliona, who dropped him a pretty little curtsy and took his arm. Together they led the procession out of the drawing room and down the stairs to the dining room at the back of the house.

As they walked he saw her looking about her with admiration.

"I told you I was eager to see inside your house when I saw the towers," she said. "I never thought that my wish would be granted so quickly."

Charles smiled as he handed her to her seat on his right.

"We often have to wait a long time before we get what we want," he replied. "So you must not miss or forget anything you are seeking just in case the next time you look for it – it has gone."

He had not meant to say such a thing, and told himself he should not have done so.

Yet somehow the words seemed to fall from his lips by themselves. He had told himself that perhaps this would be the last time visitors would see the castle as perfect as he had made it. John's winning streak would not last and either he must start selling, or find an heiress ready to sell herself for his title as he would sell himself for her money.

The thought disgusted him. It seemed degrading, especially now that he had Cliona beside him, in all her fresh beauty.

"It is wonderful, just as I knew it would be," she said. "Will you show me it all later.

"Of course I will."

'I am glad,' he thought to himself, 'she will see the castle now in its perfection just as I wanted it to be. The next time she comes, there could be empty places on the walls and furniture missing from some of the rooms.'

Either that or the house would have a new mistress.

The dining room was a solid, oak-panelled room, one end of which featured a large stone, inglenook fireplace. In the centre was a long rosewood table, surrounded by carved chairs made of the same wood. Cascading flower arrangements from the castle's gardens adorned the length of the table.

There were silver candlesticks and decanters in silver holders. The white napery gleamed, the silver and crystal shone. The china was the finest Sevres.

Charles might feel his world crumbling beneath him, but he could still provide a splendid table to delude the world.

"You are looking worried," Lady Arnfield ventured. She was on his left. "Has anything happened to one of your horses?"

"Why should you think so?" Charles asked.

"Because of the coming race meeting. You always get worried then, in case one of your horses doesn't excel itself." She spoke across the table to Cliona. "I told you about Charles's race horses, didn't I? You will see them in action very soon."

"I should love that," said Cliona, beaming.

The Hartley cook was Mrs. Watkins, wife of the butler and tonight she had outdone herself.

Never one to be behind the times, she had learned one of the new recipes that had been named after Miss Florence Nightingale, *Riz à la Soeur Nightingale*, as she proudly announced. True, her husband murmured that it was only kedgeree under another name, but nobody listened to him.

There was fresh trout, caught only that morning on the Hartley estate, gigot of lamb, followed by claret jelly, cabinet pudding, sponge cake and compôte of peaches. Each dish was served with the appropriate fine wine.

All round the table there were murmurings of admiration, and Charles knew that he could breathe again. Even if only for a little while.

At last the time came for the ladies to leave the gentlemen to their port. Nobody wanted to linger and when the port had made the rounds, they all rose to their feet with relief and headed for the music room, where Lady Hester had led the ladies.

As they walked down the passage, Charles could hear the sound of somebody singing. It was a sweet young voice, one that he had never heard before.

The men all entered the music room quietly, so as not to disturb the singer.

Lady Arnfield was sitting at the piano, playing the accompaniment, while Cliona stood beside her, singing in a pure, true voice that held everyone entranced.

It was a bright, happy song, about a girl who could not decide between three suitors. One was rich, one was handsome, and one loved her 'more than the stars'.

Her audience was smiling and joining in the chorus.

"Oh, what shall I do? What shall I do?

How do I know which choice to make?

Only one can be right for me,

But how do I know?"

Charles stayed back in the shadows as she embarked on the last verse, so that he could watch her unnoticed. At last the maiden chose the swain who loved her most.

"What shall I do? What shall I do?" Charles sang with

the others, wishing his own problems could be solved in this delightful manner.

The audience applauded heartily when Cliona had finished and Freddy bounced forward.

"I know a good song," he suggested. "It's ever so jolly. I say, you don't mind, do you?" This was to Lady Arnfield, who smiled and yielded her place at the piano. Freddy sat down and began to play. "Do you know this one?"

It was a currently popular song, and Cliona did know it. She sat down beside him at the piano and they thumped on the keys together with more vigour than skill, raising their voices in a merry duet.

Charles watched her, smiling, and was caught by surprise when she glanced up and met his eyes. Her smile matched his own, and for a moment it was as though they had excluded everyone else.

'This is my social duty,' she said to him silently. 'But I would rather be with you.'

'All I want is to get you to myself,' his eyes replied.

At last the song was over and the musicians were rewarded with eager applause. They rose and stood side by side, holding hands as he bowed and she curtsied. Then Freddy bent low over her hand and touched the back of it with his lips.

Charles decided that this had gone on long enough.

"Lady Cliona," he said, firmly engineering Freddy's departure, "you wanted to see the castle."

Lord Markham was heading for the spotlight to sing one of his funny songs. Everyone was enthusiastic, for his songs were much enjoyed in the locality. Under cover of the acclaim Charles and Cliona slipped out.

"I have never seen such a place," she sighed as she put her hand into his arm. "Other houses are just boring and ordinary, but yours looks as though it is full of dark secrets."

"Is that how you think a house should be? Full of dark secrets?" he replied.

"The darker the better," she said with theatrical relish. "And a good few ghosts."

"I'm afraid Hartley Castle has no ghosts."

"No ghosts," she cried indignantly. "Then it isn't a proper castle."

"I was afraid you might say that. The best I can offer is a few black sheep."

"That sounds a bit more encouraging."

"Come to the portrait gallery, and I'll show you."

In the great gallery he led her down the length of the portraits.

"This unpleasant looking man is the first Baron," he said, holding a lamp close. "He was a crony of Richard III, and the story goes that he was involved in the murder of the little Princes in the Tower of London."

"I don't believe it," she countered at once. "One of my ancestors was reputed to have done that, and I know of at least two others. If you believe the stories, there must have been enough villains around that night to step on each other's toes."

Charles laughed. "I've often thought the same. Let's see, who else can I find to impress you? Here's the second Countess, who was a lady in waiting to Queen Elizabeth. She was also reputed to be a poisoner. She lost several husbands in suspicious circumstances."

Cliona began to wander on ahead of him.

"Who are these lovely little boys?" she asked, stopping before a portrait.

"My father and his brother," said Charles, coming up beside her. "They were twins."

"And these?" she asked, moving on again.

"One of them is me, the other is my cousin John. We both take after our fathers, which is why we're so alike."

"Yes, for a moment I thought they were twins too. But now I look closer I can see the differences. Were you close?"

"Yes, we were," he said after a moment. "As boys we were like brothers, always getting into mischief and backing each other up." He smiled as memories of those days came back to him. "One of us would do the dirty deed and the other would be the lookout."

"What dirty deed?"

He grinned. "Any dirty deed that needed doing. We didn't care. If it got the grown-ups upset it was fun. At school they tried to split us up, thinking we were less dangerous apart. It didn't work. We just gravitated back together."

His smile faded as his memories became more intense. "He was my best and dearest friend. I told him things that I have never told anyone else. And he confided in me too. I thought I knew everything that he was thinking."

There was a long silence before she asked sympathetically, "and you didn't?"

"No," he said quietly. "I didn't."

"What happened?"

It would have been so easy to tell her all about John, but strangely he found that he just couldn't do it. Talking about his childhood had seemed to bring the old John back for a moment, bright, witty, daredevil and someone the young Charles had secretly admired.

For a moment he forgot the recent past and thought about the person who had once been closer to him than anyone in the world. The glow of that golden time lived again, and he knew he could not speak badly of John, even to her. It would have been disloyal.

Seeing her looking at him curiously, he hastened to say, "nothing really happened. We grew up and grew apart."

"But surely you could still be friends?"

"Our lives lie apart. He lives in London. It is useless to dwell on the past."

"Oh yes, I do agree," she said with quick sympathy. "Whether it was happy or sad, dwelling on it can be just as painful."

She spoke with a peculiar inflection, as though her words had a special significance, personal to herself, and he looked closely at her.

"You are so young," he said gently. "Surely there hasn't been time for your life to contain much of either?"

"It takes only a moment for happiness to be destroyed," she replied.

"You are right," he said sombrely. "And a long time for it to be created."

"Not always. It can happen in a moment, as I found by your river. A moment before I had been feeling discontented and unsettled. But then I saw this hurrying water, shining in the sun, and it seemed to speak to me, as though it was offering me a gift. And it gave me a moment of such happiness."

"I'm so glad," he said tenderly.

As they talked he had led her towards the door and out into the passage. He took her downstairs using a private staircase, rather than the main one which they had used to descend to dinner.

At the foot of the steps they paused, listening to the music that was still coming along a narrow corridor from the music room.

"We should go back to the others," he said.

"Yes, I suppose we should."

"But let me show you the garden first," he suggested, taking her hand and leading her in the other direction.

Outside, darkness had fallen. The flowers were turned to silver and the trees seemed to be hiding secrets.

"How lovely everything looks in the moonlight," said Cliona. "Sometimes I wish it could always be moonlight – soft and mysterious."

"But dangerous," he added. "Moonlight can hide so much. Isn't it better to see the truth in the sunshine?"

"But do you see it?" she asked. "I think it can be an illusion that we see better when a bright light is cast over things."

Again she spoke as though she was thinking of something personal, and Charles was moved so say,

"Why were you feeling discontented and unsettled that day by the river?"

"Oh – " she shrugged, "everything and nothing. Many people would think I was the luckiest girl in the world."

"You told me that your father died last year. I suppose that must have been very sad for you. And your mother a year earlier."

"Yes, I loved my mother very much. I loved Papa too and he really did love me." She sounded as though she was trying to persuade herself. "I know he did. It was just – he thought everything would be all right – he always thought that."

"He gambled a good deal, didn't he?" said Charles gently.

"You heard? I suppose everyone heard. That's why we moved abroad. To escape the notoriety. And it can be easier to gamble abroad."

They began to walk away from the house, deeper into the garden, finding their way by the moonlight.

"Were you very unhappy having to live away from your own country?" asked Charles.

"I didn't mind. It was a very free and easy life compared to how I would have lived in England. It was exciting too. Sometimes Papa would win a lot of money, and we would live well, and at other times he'd lose and we'd have to move out of our hotel very fast, before the bailiffs came. Sometimes we had everything and sometimes we had nothing, because Papa sold things to pay his debts."

Charles frowned, glad that the darkness was hiding his face. He found this story painful for reasons he could never have told her.

"It sounds far too exciting," he observed after a while.

"Well, to a little girl growing up it could be fun. Papa taught me all sorts of things that a young lady isn't supposed to know." She gave a little laugh. "You wouldn't believe how many card games I can play."

"Your father taught you?"

"He taught me everything. Oh dear!" she stopped with her hand over her mouth. "I promised Aunt Martha I wouldn't tell anybody. She said Papa was disreputable, and it would make people think me 'an improper person'."

"Don't worry," he said tenderly. "Your secret is safe with me."

"Oh I know that, or I wouldn't have told you. It is such a relief to be able to speak freely. You don't know what it's like having to conceal the truth of your whole existence."

"Perhaps I do," he said quietly. "But please tell me more about your life. I gather it's been like no other girl's."

"In many ways. I have met many unusual people – "

"Improper people?" he teased.

"Some of them were on the run from the law. Papa made friends with everyone. As I said, I quite enjoyed it.

But Mama was different. She didn't find it fun. She wanted a quiet, settled life in her own country, living as other women lived.

"Papa kept promising that one day soon he would win a lot of money and we could all go back to England, but it never happened, and at last Mama lost hope. He was still making promises on the day she died.

"I think that's when I grew up. Suddenly I saw that it wasn't really fun at all. Mama had pined and pined, longing for her home and her own family. And Papa had given her fine words and forgotten them five minutes later, because he was too selfish to care for anything but his own pleasures.

"Because of him she was buried in a foreign grave among strangers. And still Papa would not admit that there was anything wrong with the way we were living. He said he was giving me a good education, because I learned to speak several languages. We had friends in high society because he could charm his way wherever he went. He couldn't think what more I could want.

"And I didn't know how to tell him how much I wanted a home, certainly not in words that he could understand. And then he died when we were in Berlin, and I was left alone."

"Completely alone?" Charles echoed, aghast.

"I had my old Nanny, and she saved me. I felt quite desperate, and I prayed and prayed for something good to happen. But Tibby told me, 'It's no use sitting down and waiting for good luck to come through the window. You have to go out and find it yourself. Or create it.'

"She knew that my mother's brother was an explorer. He was usually living in a tent on the other side of the world, but he happened to be in Paris at that time, lecturing about his discoveries. Tibby said, 'we're going to Paris,' and bundled me onto a train.

"She was wonderful. In Paris we waited outside the lecture hall and when my uncle came out she just pushed me in front of him. Luckily I look very much like Mama, so he knew I was his niece. After that I stayed with him, and for a while I had a kind of home, but early this year he too died."

"That's a terrible story," Charles admitted.

"Oh no, not really, because when things were at their worst, there was always some moment of beauty to make life worthwhile. I'd be feeling weary and depressed, and I would hear a bird singing. That's why I believe in miracles. Even a little thing can be a miracle, and sometimes the little ones are the ones that matter."

He could not speak. Her simple belief in the goodness of life, her conviction that a kindly power was watching over her, made him feel that he had yielded to his own despair too readily.

And suddenly they heard a sound from the house.

Somebody was playing the violin, a gentle aching tune that reached them on the breeze. It was poignant and beautiful and they listened in silence, looking at each other in the moonlight.

She smiled at him.

"You see?" she said softly.

Turning, she began to walk away from him across the lawn, almost seeming to float. And the music drifted after her.

CHAPTER SIX

For a while Charles stayed as he was, feeling as if he was transfixed. Then he began to follow Cliona across the lawn, her pale dress just visible as it fluttered in the semi-darkness.

Between the trees and flowers he moved, until he came to a small stream where Cliona was standing, looking into the water, as he had first seen her.

It flashed through his mind that perhaps she was so fond of the water, because she was part of it herself. That somehow, if he was not careful, she would step into it and disappear.

Instead of being earth-bound and ordinary as other women were, she was mystical and not really of this world.

'I must stop thinking these absurd thoughts and be sensible,' he told himself.

But he did not want to be sensible where Cliona was concerned. He wanted to fall at her feet.

As he neared her she glanced up at him and then looked away to where the stream meandered into the trees.

"Have you found what you are looking for?" Charles asked her.

There was silence for a moment. Then she asked,

"Is that was you think I'm doing? Looking for something?"

"After what you've told me tonight, I should think you have been looking for something special all your life."

She nodded. "I've always sought something to hold onto, but I think that's true of everyone in different ways."

"Something to hold onto," he mused, "something that will guide us when we cannot guide ourselves."

He spoke very softly. As she looked up at him, he could just make out her face and sense her surprise.

"You will find it," she said in a voice that came from her heart. "Just as I did. I know that it is God himself who protects and helps us."

"I want to believe that," he burst out, "but I can't. There's no answer for me, I know that now. I search in all directions, but I know there's no hope."

She gave a gasp of horror.

"No, that's terribly wrong. You mustn't give up hope. That is the only real sin, to despair and believe that God will not help you."

Then to the Earl's surprise he felt her slip her hand into his, as she said, "you don't see it now because we're only human and we don't understand God's way, but He will show you what you are seeking."

It was as though she had the mysterious power to read his thoughts. How else could her magic be explained?

But then he knew that there was another explanation, that her magic was the oldest in the world and he had been a fool to let himself fall under her spell. For by doing so he had certainly made things worse for himself. To debt and despair he had now added the pain of a parting from a woman he loved.

A woman he loved.

No, he thought at once. *The* woman he loved.

He had loved before, or thought he had. But never like

this. Other women had charmed and excited him, but no more than that. This woman's soul spoke to his.

For what seemed like an age, he floundered in silence. At last, as if the words were torn from him, he said,

"Then I am the worst of sinners, because I do despair. There is nothing else for me. My prayers don't reach Heaven or, if they do, nobody listens to them."

Scarcely were the words out than her finger tips were across his lips. "Never say that. Never. Try to have faith."

"I have faith in you," he replied. "Only you."

"I will pray for you, just as you must pray for yourself. And you will no longer be unhappy and afraid."

She spoke in a very soft quiet voice. Yet Charles seemed to hear every word almost as if she was saying it from Heaven itself. He was in a dream, but he tried to think clearly.

"How can you know that?" he implored. "How can you be sure that what you are saying to me is the truth?"

"What I have said will come true," Cliona said in a very low voice. "I feel it in my heart and in my soul."

She turned and started to walk back the way they had come. He followed her and by the time he caught up with her she had reached the steps.

"Look at me, Cliona," he said.

She turned and gazed at him without speaking. He could just see her in the moonlight.

"You were born under a lucky star," she said. "When we met the other day, I knew as soon as you spoke to me that somehow I would be able to prevent you from suffering so much."

"How could you know that?" Charles asked.

But Cliona shook her head.

"It's a mistake to ask too much. Can you not simply trust me?"

He said hoarsely, "I would trust you more than anyone in the world."

"Look!" She pointed to the sky. "I said you were born under a lucky star. There it is, do you see it?"

Charles followed her pointing finger up into the heavens. He was standing so close to her that her sweet fragrance reached him, like the scent of fresh flowers, making him giddy with delight and desire.

"Which one?" he asked. "I can't tell."

"There! The one that's sparkling more brightly than any of the others. Can you see how it outshines them all? That is your star."

"Because you say so?" he asked tenderly.

"Because it's true." She swung round to face him. "I know. Trust me, I know. Don't you believe me?"

"I think I would believe anything you told me," he said quietly.

She smiled. The moonlight was directly on her face and he saw again how lovely she was. There was a soft glow to the pearls in her hair and about her neck, but a deeper glow in her eyes.

For a moment he just looked at her.

Then his arms seemed to move without his urging them. Suddenly they were around her, he was pulling her close, his lips seeking hers in a burning kiss.

In the past he had kissed many women. Too many, perhaps. But this was unlike anything he had experienced before. This was the kiss he had been waiting for all his life. The kiss of the one and only woman.

He felt her body soft against his and pulled her closer still, feeling that they were part of each other.

"Cliona," he murmured, kissing her again and again.

At last he drew back a little to look down on her sweet face, half expecting her to berate him for his forwardness. No gentleman kissed a girl passionately on such short acquaintance. He had proved himself a cad – that was what she would say. Then she would slap his face. And he would deserve it.

He even hoped that she would do so and startle him out of the spell in which he was helpless to do anything but pursue her like a man pursuing a pixie light through a forest.

But she did nothing. She only stood there in his arms, a look of sweet contentment on her face, half smiling at him in a way that destroyed his resolution.

A kind of madness overtook him. With a groan he gathered her against him again, raining more fierce kisses on her upturned face. For a wild, intense moment passion overcame him completely. All his honourable resolutions counted for nothing against the joy of holding this wonderful woman, feeling her lips against his, her heart beating against his own.

He could have died at that moment and counted the world well lost.

He felt her responding to him and knew that her feelings were as strong as his own. Her soft arms reached up to him and he could sense her innocent soul in the embrace she gave him.

She had no false modesty, he knew that at once. No pretence of reluctance in order to inflame him. No coquettish feminine tricks to lure him on and make a fool of him. Everything in her was honest and true. If she loved a man she would be too generous to deny it in thought, word or deed. For a blissful moment everything in him rejoiced in that knowledge.

But then he was swept by a black sense of his own

dishonest behaviour.

He could not marry her. He had told himself that and he knew it to be true. He had vowed, too, to kill the attraction between them and kill his own rapidly growing feelings for her, because they could not be pursued with honour.

And what was he doing?

Behaving in a way that would compromise her if it were known. Risking the destruction of her spotless reputation for the gratification of his own feelings.

He was disgusted with himself.

Taking a deep breath, he took hold of her arms and pushed her away from him.

"No!" he said hoarsely.

He had a blinding glimpse of her face, the large eyes gazing at him in troubled disbelief.

"No," he said again. "This cannot happen. It's unforgivable."

He meant that his own behaviour was unforgivable, but he knew she had not interpreted it like that.

"I don't – understand," she said softly.

"Of course not. You're too young and innocent. I blame myself. I had no right – "

"Oh is that all?" she asked, her face lightening. "But if I give you the right – "

He turned sharply away to hide the leap of hope and temptation in his eyes. Why must she be such a darling, so ready to love him?

"You imagine it's that easy? We've met twice, and you think if a man kisses you in the moonlight that means he's a man of honour? You know nothing about men and nothing about me. You should be more careful."

She stared at him. He could not look at that gaze lest he would see too clearly that she was suffering. He couldn't bear her to be hurt, but he went on hurting her anyway, hurling cruel, insulting words at her, hoping to turn her against him so that she might never tempt him again.

If only he could tell her that he was torturing himself as much as her and doing it for her sake.

"I thought I did know you," Cliona said in a dazed voice. "As soon as we met I felt you were good and kind – "

"A very common feminine mistake, to read too much into too little. You trusted me too easily. Doesn't this prove it? No man who was good and kind would be here with you, talking like this."

He heard her gasp of pain and it nearly broke him, but he drove himself on.

"You're a very sweet but naïve girl. I took advantage of you, but I won't do so any more. Someone should have warned you. I'm not a man of good reputation where women are concerned."

"Is that what – ?" Her hand flew to her mouth as she bit back the words.

"What?" he asked, regarding her and longing with all his heart to take her in his arms and kiss her hurt away. "What were you going to say?"

"Nothing – nothing, I just – it was only – I misunderstood."

He could hear the tears in her voice and hated himself with a loathing so intense he could almost taste it. He knew he had given her pain that was almost past bearing, but he could see no other way of saving her from him. How could he blurt out the truth? How could he say –

'I need a great heiress, someone with far more money than you could possibly have. And so I will kill the beauty that has arisen between us, so that it can never weaken my resolve.'

Impossible.

And equally impossible to add,

'If I have to break your heart, it is only to protect you from my worst self. My own heart is already breaking at the thought of turning away from the finest gift life will ever offer me.'

He pulled himself together, and spoke to her formally.

"Lady Cliona, I must ask you to forgive me. I have behaved as no man should behave to a lady who is a guest under his roof. I forgot the courtesy that was due to you. I can only assure you that such rudeness will never happen again."

"Stop!" she cried wildly, "Stop, stop! Don't talk to me in that horrid, dead voice – as though there had been nothing between us – "

"But there can be nothing between us, for reasons that I cannot explain to you. It was wrong – very wrong – for me to – " he stopped with a shudder.

In the silence he could sense her waiting for him to finish, hoping against all hope to take some comfort from his final words.

"It was wrong of me," he said again heavily.

Her head went up. She was a girl of spirit.

"In that case my Lord, I am surprised that you did what you knew to be wrong," she said defiantly.

"You have every right to be angry with me. The only explanation I can give is that I – a momentary weakness – "

"But now you have managed to overcome it?" she asked fiercely.

"Yes, I had no right to – "

He gave up trying to put it into words and reluctantly

met her gaze. Her eyes were full of anger, bitterness, contempt, and he tried to tell himself that it was better that way.

"Please forgive me," he said at last. "And be kind enough to forget that this ever happened."

"I will gladly forget," she said in a firm voice. "I will try to forget everything about this evening. I will forget that I ever met you."

But she could not sustain her anger against her misery. The next moment she dropped her face into her hands with a sob.

For Charles the temptation to enfold her in his arms was unbearable. In another minute he would weaken.

"I think you should go in now," he said in a jerky voice. "I will follow later. Let us hope that nobody saw us."

She lowered her hands and he saw the sparkle of tears in her eyes, and the tremor that went through her slight body. The next moment she was running away from him like a gazelle. He watched her go, feeling that all life was over for him.

"Forgive me," he whispered. "My darling – try to forgive me."

*

Cliona ran to within a few yards of the steps that led down to the lawn from the French windows of the music room. Then she pulled herself up short, realising how impossible it would be for her to burst through those windows, with all the attention she would attract.

She leaned against the wall, heaving with distress, trying to control the tears that poured down her cheeks. For a few blinding minutes she had been surrounded by love, blessed by love.

She knew the world would say that she had behaved

disgracefully, going off alone with him, kissing him on such short acquaintance, abandoning maidenly modesty for the joy of being in his arms.

But her heart had instinctively trusted him. It had told her that his feelings for her were sincere, and she could put her hand into his and her heart into his keeping without fear.

And then her trust had been thrown cruelly back into her face. One moment he had taken her into his arms. She had sensed his passion with her own rising to meet his.

More than that, she had felt his aching need for her and his readiness to yield to that need. But the next moment he had lashed her with scorn for her shameless behaviour.

'Not a man of good reputation where women are concerned.'

Those were his own words about himself. And how could she doubt them, coming from such a source?

She had been warned. The conversation she had overheard between her aunt and uncle had hinted at just such a thing. And she had been intrigued to the point of seeking him out next morning, riding onto his land and letting him find her.

It had been part of a game, the kind that young maidens played all the time while they prepared for the great decisions of their lives. Behind the façade of etiquette they flirted, laughed, teased and loved. How else were they to discover what they needed to know before the final choice was made?

But it had ceased to be a game when she met a man whose smiles concealed sadness, and sensed the unspoken burden that came near to crushing him. After that she had cared only for becoming the one who eased his pain.

Because of that she had opened her arms to him, in love and total trust.

And been brutally snubbed.

The steps outside the French windows made a semi-circle, so she could sit down on them by the wall, out of sight of those within. It was there that Freddy found her a few minutes later.

"I say, I wondered where you'd vanished to. Have you been out here on your own all this time?"

"It's nice out here alone," she said, not answering directly. "I can sit and listen to the music in peace. That violin solo was lovely."

"Is that was made you cry?"

"I'm not crying," she said firmly.

Freddy said nothing. Beneath his light-hearted manner, he had a good deal of insight.

After a while, he said,

"Perhaps we should go in now. People will wonder where you are."

"Are you worried about my reputation?" she asked in a wobbly voice.

"Lord no! Your reputation's safe enough with me. Everyone knows I'm just an idiot and they will say, 'Oh, she's only been with old Freddy.' I'm like a carpet slipper, ma'am, I do assure you."

She managed a shaky laugh.

"In that case, let's go in together."

"The story of my life," he sighed, helping her to her feet. "Pretty girls are always ready to take my arm because they know I'm safe. Insulting really."

"Dear Freddy, I promise you, one day soon, mothers will be warning their daughters not to be alone with 'that dangerous man'."

"Really ma'am? I say, just think of that!"

Together they went inside.

Charles, watching them from the shadow of the trees, gave silent thanks to his cousin for protecting his beloved. He waited ten minutes before entering the music room through another door. Cliona and Freddy were sitting at the piano in another rousing duet.

She sang with a smile on her face, and raised her voice in the chorus as though she hadn't a care in the world. Now and then she and her musical partner exchanged smiles, and nobody could have told that only a few minutes earlier she had been distraught.

'What courage!' Charles thought in admiration. 'No self-pity or airs to make herself interesting. She'll fly her brave pennants before the entire world. But why the devil couldn't I have handled it better?'

The song came to an end with the performers collapsing against each other in mirth. Everyone applauded them, including their host who came forward from his place by the door.

"Freddy you dog, trust you to bag the guest of honour for yourself. Lady Cliona, I apologise for my cousin. I hope he hasn't been boring you."

"On the contrary, I have found Mr. Mason's company most welcome," she said in her gentle voice that thrilled his senses.

He winced and braced himself for the reproach in her eyes, but she was looking at some point just beyond his shoulder.

"I suppose we should be going," said Lady Arnfield. "Charles dear, it has been such a lovely evening."

There was a general murmur of agreement and a rustle of skirts as everyone rose to take their leave.

The polite words were said, "Charming – you must dine with us – so good to see you – we look forward to the races – "

They were moving out into the hall. Servants brought cloaks, gloves and top hats. Charles, Lady Hester and the Countess moved among the guests, murmuring courtesies.

Charles bid goodnight to Sir Kenton and Lady Arnfield. Cliona inclined her head, a meaningless smile on her lips and again her eyes did not meet his.

But when Freddy took her hand she smiled at him and murmured gently, "thank you, Freddy."

Lady Markham extended her hand in farewell.

"Such a delightful evening – good heavens! What was that?"

Heads turned at the sound of wheels on the drive, voices, feet descending and approaching the front door.

"Somebody made a mistake about the time," said Lord Markham jovially. "No use turning up now, what?"

"Who is missing?" the Countess hooted. "I thought everyone was here."

"Everybody is here," said Charles. "This is something unexpected. I do hope it isn't bad news."

Watkins moved loftily towards the front door, opened it and stood back to reveal the newcomer.

Gradually a silence fell over the guests assembled in the hall as they saw who was there.

The Countess gasped.

Lady Hester's hand flew to her mouth.

Standing in the doorway, elegant, handsome and composed, stood John Baxter.

CHAPTER SEVEN

After the first thunderstruck moment, Charles forced himself to behave normally. Of those present, he was sure most would have heard of his cousin John, but some of them would not know him by sight.

"John," he said, in a neutral voice. "What an unexpected pleasure."

"It's just like your generosity to say so, Charles," replied John, advancing into the hall. "But I doubt there's much pleasure for you. I didn't treat you well the last time I was here, did I? I wouldn't blame you for throwing me out."

"Of course I'm not going to do that."

John extended his hand.

"Will you shake my hand then? Say I am forgiven and let bygones be bygones?"

Charles had no choice but to do so. It was either that or risk an open scandal. Besides, although confused and baffled by his behaviour, he was by no means reluctant. His heart was warm and his nature not quarrelsome. Whatever John might be up to, Charles was glad of a truce.

The cousins shook hands. John's whole manner was frank, manly and attractive. The onlookers were agreeably impressed, as they could hardly fail to be, by the picture of humility on the one side and graciousness on the other.

Two such handsome young men, so alike, so splendid!

That was what they thought.

With the same quiet air John kissed his grandmother, then his aunt. They embraced him warmly, and Charles could see that they at least were made happy by this visit and by his manner.

"Forgive me for taking you by surprise while you have guests," John said meekly to Charles. "It's outrageous of me. I'll retire quietly."

"Stay and be introduced first," said Charles agreeably. "Lord and Lady Markham, this is my cousin John. Vicar – "

With a modest, agreeable air, John began to do the rounds of the guests, paying each of them a flattering attention that suggested he had been waiting just for this moment. To remarks about his likeness to his cousin, he smiled as though hearing them for the first time instead of the thousandth.

The Arnfields had met him before and knew the story of his behaviour, yet even they were briefly melted by his charm, which, as Charles knew, was considerable when he put his mind to it.

"It's so nice to see you again," he told them. "Sir Kenton, I recall the privilege of riding one of your horses some months back. It has remained one of my most pleasant memories."

"Ah, you mean Sabre," exclaimed Sir Kenton, softened by any reference to his horses. "Fine animal, but not everyone can ride him as you did."

"You are too kind."

He saw Cliona looking at John with a slight frown on her enchanting face, and knew that the moment could not be put off any longer.

"Lady Cliona," he said formally, "my cousin, John Baxter. John, Lady Cliona Locksley."

"Your servant, ma'am."

"Sir," she murmured.

"I'll have your bags taken up to your room, John," said Charles abruptly.

"That's very kind of you, cousin," said John. "Lady Cliona." He bowed.

She returned a small curtsy and made for the door with her uncle and aunt. It was the signal for everyone to leave.

"You've been a very bad boy," the Countess told John as soon as they were alone. "Come to my room. I have strong things to say to you."

"Yes, Grandmama," he said meekly.

"What are you up to, John?" asked Freddy darkly. "You don't fool me with this meek and mild manner."

"I never expected you to believe me, Freddy," said John.

"You think you're going to get away with it?"

"Of course he isn't going to get away with it," said the Countess. "He has behaved very badly, and I shall tell him so."

She departed up the stairs with Lady Hester and John.

"Much good that will do!" Freddy said wrathfully.

"Hush, Freddy," said Charles. "I'm as suspicious as you, but let us wait and see what happens. It gives his grandmother pleasure."

"And what about you? How can you take him back after he pulled a gun on you?" For Charles had wryly confided that story to Freddy the previous day.

"How could I turn him out? He is still my cousin. Besides, he clearly has something on his mind, and I'll feel safer when I know what it is."

It was a couple of hours before he saw John again.

During that time his cousin had visited the ladies, meekly endured a lecture from the Countess with occasional interventions from Lady Hester. He had followed this with an ample supper, during which he consumed half the contents of a brandy decanter.

He then carried the rest to the library where, as expected, he found Charles and Freddy. Freddy, sprawled in a chair eyed him with disfavour. Charles, his feet up on the leather sofa, saw the decanter and held out his glass.

John filled it, then Freddy's, and sat down.

"It was bad form of me to arrive like that, wasn't it?" he asked. "Uninvited and walking in without a by-your-leave, when you had guests. But you see, I was afraid that if I wrote first you would refuse to see me. Not that I blame you, you understand. My behaviour last time we met was appalling."

"True," Charles replied without heat.

"If it had been me I'd have turned the gun back on you and shot you down like a dog," Freddy said frankly.

"Then I can only be thankful I had the good sense to stay away from you," observed John wryly. "What a violent young devil you are!"

"*I'm* violent?" said Freddy in disgust. "It wasn't me who pulled a gun on Charles."

"Stop being so melodramatic, Freddy," said Charles wearily. "I'm sorry I told you about it now. It was only a popgun and he didn't fire it."

"He would have done," said Freddy.

"Yes, I think I would," John reflected. "I was mad, you see, mad with rage. Now I've had time to calm down, I am so glad I didn't."

"Thank you," said Charles ironically.

"You did me a good turn, Charles, forcing me to take

responsibility for my own actions. In the past you've given in to me too easily. This time you refused and it was right. You should have done so before."

"I have done so before," Charles observed. "It never produced this reaction. Instead I was vilified until I gave in."

"Because I knew you *would* give in. But this time I was thrown back on my own resources and it did me a world of good."

"For the love of Heaven!" Freddy murmured in disgust.

"No, let him talk, Freddy," said Charles, grinning. "It's entertaining if nothing else. Have a care, John. I've known you all your life, remember? I know how good you are at acting a role when it suits you."

"I can think of a few times when it suited you as well," said John, also grinning. "When we were in trouble as boys, who was it who always talked us out of it?"

"You," said Charles with a careless wave of the hand. "You always had the gift of a silver tongue. I've never denied that. But then, it was always you who got us into trouble in the first place!"

"I was more ingenious than you," John agreed. "And I had what every true villain needs – the conviction that I could get away with it. You never believed you could. You were always wondering what would happen."

"Yes, that was it," murmured Charles. "Do you still remember that time we raided Farmer Jacob's orchard – ?"

"And he came rampaging up to the house," John took up the story. "And we went to the window in the loft and dropped apples on his head. But that wasn't as good as when we – "

Freddy listened to these reminiscences, aghast at the way Charles was softening. Had he forgotten John's behaviour? He tried to signal to him behind John's back, reminding him of what he had suffered, but Charles seemed happy to let it go. For an hour the two cousins swapped stories of childhood delinquency.

Freddy watched in silence. He was beginning to appreciate something that Charles had told him, but which he had never understood before. These two had once been truly friends, before jealousy and the lust for money had overtaken John, and that, in losing him, Charles had suffered a bereavement like a death. Now he was like a man being revisited by a much loved ghost.

"Remember that cook – what was her name? – anyway she was going to make apple turnovers – " This was Charles's contribution.

"And we raided the kitchen and stripped it clean of apples – "

"I let the chickens out and they got into the kitchen garden and pecked all the vegetables," Charles remembered.

"You can't count that," John objected.

"Why can't I?"

"Because you did it by accident."

"Does that matter?"

"Of course. It only counts if it was malice aforethought," John asserted, refilling his glass.

"I never was much good at malice aforethought," mused Charles. "I was better at blundering idiocy."

"That's true," agreed John. He regarded the brandy decanter with surprise. "This is empty."

"It's been empty for some time," Charles pointed out. "Freddy found us another one in the cupboard."

"So he did. Where is it?"

"That's empty too," said Freddy, speaking slowly from a feeling that the world would float away if he didn't keep tight hold of it.

"You're drunk old fellow," Charles informed him amiably.

Freddy considered this. "Do you really think so?"

"Sure of it."

But Freddy wanted a second opinion. "John, am I drunk?"

But the only answer was a faint snore from the chair opposite him, where John lay with his head back.

"No use asking him," Charles said wisely. "He's drunker than you are."

Freddy thought about this.

"Nobody's drunker than I am," he said at last.

Charles hauled himself reluctantly to his feet and went over to where John lay sleeping.

"John." He touched his shoulder. "John. Time to go to bed."

There was no movement from his cousin who lay, as relaxed as a child, all care wiped from his face. Suddenly it was possible to discern the charming young man that nature had meant him to be before bitterness and jealousy had claimed him.

Looking at Charles's sad face, Freddy saw that he had been affected by the memories tonight had brought back.

'But it's more than that,' he thought. 'Something else has happened. Something he can't bear.'

"Let's get him to bed," suggested Charles.

Between them they hauled John to his feet and assisted him to the door. Through the darkened house they half dragged him, until they reached his room, where they found John's valet, Raskin, waiting up for him.

"I'll take him now, my Lord," he said softly to Charles.

Watching the easy way the man steered John to the

bed, laid him down and began to remove his shoes, Charles was struck by an idea.

"Do you do this very often?" he asked.

"Pretty often, my Lord. When he wins and when he loses. He had a huge win yesterday. Very gratifying, if I may say so. Dead to the world for hours, he was." Raskin sounded proud of his master's achievements.

"So there's part of the answer," said Charles to Freddy as they walked away. "He had a huge win, so my refusal of cash no longer rankles."

"And he thought it wise to make his peace in readiness for the next time," said Freddy. "Don't trust him, Charles. Nothing has really changed. He'll spend his winnings and be back."

"I know he will. Don't fret my lad. I may have let myself grow a little sentimental tonight, but it doesn't mean I am completely off-guard. Goodnight."

Once in his own room Charles sent his valet away and removed his coat, not sure whether to be glad or sorry that the evening was over. He had been glad to prolong the last part of it in his cousin's company, because that way he was spared from having to reflect too deeply on what had happened earlier.

But there was to be no escape for him now. He could still see Cliona's face, eagerly willing to give him her love and then distraught as he rebuffed her. He closed his eyes, trying to banish her, but she would not be banished.

He relived the scene endlessly, trying to manage everything better and to word his refusal more sensitively, but it was useless. He had meant to be kind and caring, but in the end he had been stupid, clumsy and cruel. The stain on his conscience would not be wiped away.

In his mind he saw again her tears, sparkling like the star she had shown him, promising him that it was all his.

His heart seemed to constrict within him. With her sweet generosity she had tried to restore his faith. She had even kissed him. And he had broken her heart.

No. He resisted that thought. She was young and beautiful. Admirers would crowd around her. She would soon forget him and love another. It was his own heart that was fatally wounded.

He pulled open his window and leaned out, trying to find that perfect glittering star that shone so much more brightly than the others.

But dawn was breaking, and he could no longer see the stars.

*

Cliona had always risen early. When you had lived one step ahead of the bailiffs, it became a necessary habit. The morning after the dinner party she was up at her normal time, so that her uncle and aunt noticed nothing unusual in her behaviour.

Nor were they surprised when she elected to take her normal ride, and since they were now coming under her sway they did not object when she left her groom behind.

She did not delude herself about the purpose of her ride. She went straight to the place in the wood where she had first met Charles. If only he would come in search of her today, she could discover the truth about his strange attitude and win from him his acknowledgement in words of what she had sensed in his lips, his arms and the beating of his heart.

If not –

But she refused to consider that, lest her anguish should be too great to bear.

She waited half an hour while the bright day about her grew steadily bleaker and the ache in her heart became unbearable. But then, just as she was about to give up and ride home, she saw him riding between the trees, the slanting sunbeams touching his hair.

Gladness flooded her. She almost called his name. The next moment she was glad she had not done so.

It was not Charles, but John.

She sat there, waiting for the beating of her heart to subside, reflecting bitterly on the family likeness that had cruelly deceived her. By the time he reached her, she was in full command of herself.

John had observed her from afar and blessed the luck that had thrown him this chance. Approaching her, he smiled, on his best behaviour.

"Lady Cliona," he said, doffing his hat. "Your servant, ma'am."

She inclined her head with a little gracious gesture. For the moment she was terribly tempted to ask him about Charles, but she remained resolute. She would wear her heart on her sleeve for no man.

"I gather I missed an excellent evening last night", John ventured.

"Yes, it was a pity that you arrived late. We were having such fun making music."

"I never thought of my cousin as a man for music."

"He is certainly not a performer," she agreed. "Perhaps he likes listening. Since I have only just met him I could not say. Will your visit be a long one? I do hope so."

"How kind of you. I hope it may. I certainly mean to be here for the race meeting next week. It's always a big occasion."

"So my Uncle Kenton tells me. I gather there is great rivalry between himself and Lord Hartley."

He laughed. "Immense. Last year one of Sir Kenton's

horses won a race that my cousin was expected to win. It was practically pistols at dawn, but they remembered in time that they are the best of friends."

She was managing to cope better, she thought, now that the first shock was over. It was not really possible to confuse them. Their builds were similar, their hair identical, but their faces were merely alike, not the same.

But still, she could have wished they looked just a little more different.

They didn't act alike. She soon realised that John was putting himself out to be charming. Charles was not charming or not deliberately so. He was slightly gruff and burdened with care, so that she yearned to protect him.

John did not inspire her with protective feelings. He was too much at ease for that. But he was pleasing company for a while, so she smiled and turned her horse to ride with him.

She chattered, not gently and sincerely as she had with Charles, but brightly like a magpie, laughing a little too merrily at John's witticisms, and capping them with some of her own, so that he too roared with laughter.

They looked so attractive, so right together. Anybody would have thought they presented a delightful pair.

But the man watching them from a short distance away did not think so. He sat very still on Lightning, scowling as they cantered away from him. Whatever might have been his object in coming to the wood, he knew now that it was pointless.

How could he have imagined her broken-hearted or pining for him? It was laughable. *He* was laughable, a clown stumbling through the world, doing nothing right. He knew it now.

He waited until they had vanished from his sight. Then he galloped back to Hartley Castle.

To Charles's relief John did not demand to be entertained, seeming quite capable of occupying himself. He went out every day, mounted on one of the best horses and Charles heard of his activities only by rumour.

In three days they had only one real conversation in which John said casually,

"You probably think I've come here to agitate you about money again. Well, I haven't. I have sorted my own affairs out, as you told me to."

"You raised all that money?" asked Charles in some surprise.

"I won a great deal playing cards one evening. More than I could have hoped. It doesn't solve the entire problem, of course, but I'll take care of that myself too. You've been dashed good to me, old man, and very patient. But it's all over now, I swear it."

"I'm glad to hear it," said Charles shortly.

"You sound as if you're still angry. I suppose I can't blame you after all I've done. But I swear things will be different from now on. Will you shake my hand?"

Charles regarded his cousin's outstretched hand with distaste. But to refuse was impossible, and so he put out his own and offered the briefest possible shake.

But John clasped Charles's hand between his own two and shook it long and heartily.

"Dashed good of you, old man. I won't forget this." He seemed on the verge of tears.

"No need to make a fuss," said Charles gruffly. "Go and visit our grandmother. She was asking for you."

When John had departed, Freddy, who had been watching the scene with disgusted fascination, said scathingly,

"Did you hear that noise he makes as he moves?"

"Noise?"

"A creaking noise."

"Now you mention it, yes I did hear something of the kind. Why should John creak?"

"Corsets."

"Corsets?"

"Haven't you noticed that his waist doesn't bulge as it used to?"

"Yes – but why?"

"He's after an heiress. That's what he means by solving his problems. And I'll tell you another thing. My valet has been talking to his valet, and Raskin has some interesting tales to tell."

"About corsets presumably."

"That too. But also about this big win at cards. That was a very fishy business."

"You mean he didn't win at all?"

"Oh, he won all right. But not money. Title deeds."

"What do you mean?"

"Someone staked the title deeds to his home, and that's what John won. Ever since, the loser has been going round screaming that John cheated, but there's no proof."

"Oh dear God!" Charles groaned. "Is there no end to it? If he doesn't disgrace the family one way, he does it in another. Where will it end?"

"I told you, it will end in a great heiress. He's set on it."

"Then why come here? There are no great heiresses in this part of the world."

"But there are. According to Raskin he's set his cap at Lady Cliona, *one of the wealthiest women in the country.*"

There was a silence. Then Charles gave a hard, mirthless laugh.

"You're out of your mind, Freddy. Lady Cliona is practically penniless."

"Did she tell you that?"

"Yes – well – as good as. Her father gambled away every penny and left her stranded when he died. If it hadn't been for her uncle – "

"Exactly," said Freddy triumphantly. "The uncle, who amassed a huge fortune travelling all over the world – China, Egypt, India, America. Apparently he had a passion for gold and collected it everywhere.

"When he died he left a vast collection of solid gold pieces. Some went to museums, but the bulk was left to Lady Cliona. They say she's worth about two million pounds. I say Charles, are you all right? You've gone a very nasty colour."

"My God!" Charles groaned. "What have I done? What have I done?"

He sat down and buried his head in his hands.

"Well, what *have* you done, old chap? Nothing dreadful, surely?"

"Nothing dreadful? Only the worst thing in the world."

"Would this have anything to do with the other night?"

"What do you mean?"

"The night of the party. I found her sitting outside on the steps, crying. What had you done to make her cry, Charles?"

"Mind your own business!" said Charles savagely.

"As bad as that, eh?"

"Look, my family has been at me to marry money and I had finally come to believe that it was my duty. I had no

100

right to go into the garden with a girl I believed penniless, no right to – no right to do any of the things that I did."

"What exactly did you do?"

"Freddy, I'm warning you – !"

"All right, all right. I suppose you made love to her and then had an attack of scruples. The question is, was she crying about the love-making or the scruples?"

"One more word out of you – "

"My guess is, the scruples," said Freddy, hopping nimbly out of reach. "So why worry? All you have to do is go back to her and explain that you got everything wrong."

"Really? And what do I tell her now, Freddy? Do I say that I turned away from her when I thought she had no money, but now I know she's fabulously rich, *that's all right?* Could any man with a vestige of honour say such a thing to any woman, even one he didn't – ?"

"Even one he didn't love?" asked Freddy.

"Never mind that. Don't you see that this news has put it out of my power ever to speak to her about love?"

"No I don't see it. Either you love the girl or you don't."

"But how can she ever believe that now? You suggest I parade myself before her as a common fortune hunter?" Charles asked and added sadly,

"It's too late, Freddy. Now she can never trust a word I say. Everything is over."

CHAPTER EIGHT

From his place of concealment in the trees, Charles watched while the front door of the Lord Lieutenant's house opened and John emerged with Cliona. A groom had brought his horse around. John took the reins and waited until the man had departed before taking Cliona's hand and lifting it to his lips.

He kissed the back of her hand, then, before Charles's furious eyes, turned it over and kissed the palm. Lightning stirred as his rider's knees tightened involuntarily.

"Steady, boy," said Charles gently.

Since the morning he had come across John and Cliona in the wood and watched them in secret, he had taken care never to do so again. But today it was essential.

He kept well back until John had galloped past him. Cliona was still there in the doorway, watching the departing figure. She looked enchanting in a dark grey riding habit that showed off her tiny waist and flared hips.

They must have been riding together, Charles thought. And when the ride was over they had come back here to spend time talking and enjoying each other's company.

How long had they been together? How many times had he kissed that precious hand?

And she had permitted it.

Then he had arrived not a moment too soon.

Now he blamed himself for taking so long. He should have warned her the moment he knew John's plans. But he had foolishly imagined that Lady Cliona possessed too much delicacy to allow attentions from such a character.

Then his heart insisted on absolving her. She did not know the truth about John and for that, he himself was to blame.

Now he must act.

But a shock awaited him. When he had handed Lightning to the groom who came running out, and knocked at the front door, it was opened by Davis, the Kenton's steward, who knew him well. But instead of standing back for him to pass, Davis shifted uncomfortably from foot to foot, and stood in the doorway, blocking his entrance.

"I have come to see Lady Cliona Locksley," explained Charles.

"I am sorry, my Lord, but Lady Cliona is not at home."

"What do you mean, not at home?" Charles demanded in outrage. "I have just seen her. I know she's here."

"Yes, my Lord," said Davis miserably. "But she is not at home."

"Don't talk such rubbish to me. You know who I am. Stand aside."

"I'm sorry, my Lord. I have my orders."

"Whose orders?"

"Her Ladyship's."

"And is she 'not at home' to everybody?" asked Charles dangerously.

Davis gulped.

"No, my Lord. Just to your Lordship."

He looked so miserable that Charles took pity on him. Stepping inside he lifted Davis bodily out of his way.

"Now Lady Cliona cannot blame you," he said. "Just tell her it was my fault."

"Yes, my Lord. Whatever your Lordship says."

The door to the drawing room was ajar and through the small gap he could see her. Wasting no time on niceties he marched in, shut the door behind him and said,

"What the devil do you mean by refusing to see me?"

"I should have thought my meaning was all too evident," she said coolly. "Please leave at once."

"I will do no such thing."

"Then I shall summon the servants to eject you."

"If you mean Davis, I don't think he'll risk it. Don't be a goose. The people in this house have known me for years. None of them is going to touch me on your orders."

"Then I am asking you to leave," she said with dignity.

"When I have said what I came to say."

"Be good enough to say it and leave."

"Hang it, Cliona, stop talking to me like an offended dowager."

She turned on him.

"Sir, you have informed me that you are not a man of good reputation where women are concerned, and now I see it to be true. You have forced yourself into my presence and I find myself alone with you despite my protests."

"Cliona – "

But she had become an avenging fury. "May I remind you, sir, that it was you yourself who told me that '*I should be more careful*'. That was your way of calling me shameless, I suppose – "

"It was not – "

"Well, I am trying to be careful, but it's very hard when I am assaulted by a rude man, who cares nothing if he compromises me – "

She broke off abruptly and turned away before her voice wobbled too obviously.

"I apologise if you feel I have behaved badly," said Charles stiffly. "I did not mean to come here – I tried to avoid it – "

"How considerate of you!" she said angrily.

"I came because it is my duty. I have to warn you – for your own sake – I cannot leave you in ignorance of – " he took a deep breath. "I came about my cousin John."

She stared at him.

"I saw him leaving here today," Charles stumbled on, driven by his love and his despair, getting the words wrong, knowing it, but unable to stop.

"I saw him depart and I saw how he kissed your hand and I have to warn you not to encourage his attentions."

A pall of icy dignity seemed to settle over Cliona.

"You have already indicated that I am not good enough for you – "

"I never – "

"Now you wish me to know that I am not good enough for any of your family. Very well, you have said what you came to say. Now I demand that you leave."

"Why must you misunderstand me at every turn?" he cried. "Of course you are good enough for my family. You are far too good – "

He checked himself and sighed despondently.

"I am doing this very badly. Just let me speak, and then I'll leave you alone, I promise."

He could not bear to meet her eyes and see in them the look that set him at a distance, so he turned away and went to stand in the window.

"When we first met," he said, speaking with difficulty, "you knew at once that I was troubled. It was true, but I didn't tell you what the trouble was. I wish now that I had."

"Why should it make a difference – *now?*"

"Because the trouble was John. *Is* John. I told you that our fathers were twins. You saw the portraits. His father grew up with the idea that he was a dispossessed heir. He passed that notion on to John, who decided that I owed him something. In fact, he thinks I owe him everything."

He turned to face her.

"He spends money like water and tosses the bills to me. I have always paid them because the alternative was seeing John put into a debtor's gaol, and for the sake of my family name and the feelings of our grandmother, I could not allow it. He knows that. He counts on it. He spends and spends and has brought me to the edge of destruction.

"Now I have to think of money, not for myself but for the sake of those who depend on me and to preserve my heritage. I have to think of it all the time. I cannot allow myself to think of anything else.

"The other evening, I shouldn't have gone out into the garden with you. I had no right, knowing that marriage between us was impossible. My only excuse is that I was weak. I longed for you and I – "

Her eyes were fixed on him in tense yearning, and he knew that her anger had melted. Now she was waiting, longing for him to say he loved her. But he could not say it.

"I was not honest with you," he said. "If I had been – things might be different between us now."

She was softening now, regarding him so sweetly that it almost broke him. But for her sake he would not yield.

"But I was a coward," he continued sharply. "I couldn't bear to tell you the truth, and so I put a barrier between us that can never be torn down."

"Charles, you're frightening me."

"There's no need for you to be frightened. But let me tell you quickly, so that you can despise me as I despise myself, and then let there be an end."

His features stood out lividly as he spoke, so that she had an impression of a man beset by horror. He was like someone who had looked into hell, and still carried the mark.

"I could never despise you. I lo- "

But she was silenced by his hand over her lips.

"Don't say that," he begged. "Don't love me, or if you do, don't tell me. Spare me the knowledge that I have done you that harm. On my life, I never meant to hurt you. I did not understand until it was too late."

"But how can it be too late?" Her eyes widened. "Are you telling me that you are married already? You have a secret wife?"

"Of course not" he almost shouted. "How can you think that of me even for a moment?"

"Because you are determined to make me think ill of you, but you will not tell me why. So far all I know is that you kissed me and then rejected me. You made me feel that I had behaved badly, that in some way I wasn't good enough – "

"No, never that," he groaned. "It was not you who wasn't good enough, but me. If you had known what a mean wretch I am, and how unworthy of you – " He shook his head like a tormented bear trying to shake off wasps.

Cliona stood very still. Her face was pale as she said,

"Very well, tell me what a mean wretch you are, and let me judge for myself."

"I have a duty to my family, a duty to marry money. I cannot think of love. I have to marry for money and secure the family's future."

107

Silence.

At last he looked at her. Instead of the contempt he had expected, there was a little frown of concentration on her forehead.

"You mean it doesn't matter what the woman is like, as long as she has money?" she asked at last.

He winced, but answered, "That's right."

"She could be old and ugly, with bad teeth, as long as she has money?"

He closed his eyes. "Yes."

Cliona's answer, like everything about her, was unexpected. She walked to the mirror over the mantelpiece and looked earnestly into it. She then turned back to him.

"You cannot see any lines yet," she announced with an air of triumph, "and I don't have bad teeth."

He felt a lump in his throat. "Please – " he implored huskily. "Don't."

"But I do have money."

"I know that now. I didn't know it then. When I turned from you in the garden, it was because I thought you were penniless."

"But how could you? My wealth has been like a curse dogging me."

"But I knew nothing of it until I learned of John's plans to pursue you for it. You told me about your life with your father, how he'd gambled away every penny. I didn't know your uncle had left you a fortune in gold.

"If I *had* known that, I should have pursued you. There, now you know the worst of me. I'm a miserable fortune hunter. I have to be. I don't like it. I loathe myself for it, but it's what I am."

"I don't believe that" she replied. "Why must you judge yourself so harshly? Charles, in the short season I had in London I met fortune hunters of many kinds. I can pick them out. I have heard every plausible story, every lie. You don't belong in that crowd. I know you don't."

She gave a shaky smile and laid her hand on his arm.

"If you were a true fortune hunter you would have asked me to marry you by now."

He stared.

"Do you think I could ever ask you, after this?"

"But if you need my money – "

"Anybody's money but yours," he said violently. "I've behaved badly to you, but I will not sink to those depths."

"Have you behaved badly?" she asked, a little wistfully.

"I should never have kissed you, but I couldn't help myself. You were like balm to my soul. I had forgotten that such a woman as you existed – if I had ever really known."

He moved closer to her.

"Do you understand what I am? A man who fled you when he thought you were penniless, but had second thoughts when he realised you were rich? Do you think I can ever pay court to you in those circumstances? Do you think I could live with you, always fearing to look into your eyes lest I see the scorn I deserve?"

"But – you've explained it all to me now – "

"Clever words to beguile you. Don't trust them. Don't trust me." His voice grew harder as he lashed himself with derision. "I always knew how to make women fall in love with me. That's an uncomfortable truth that you should consider. In your case I decided that an appearance of honesty would be the best way to allay your suspicions."

Cliona's eyes were enormous in her pale face.

"Is that really the truth?"

"No, of course it isn't," he cried. "But how can you tell? It could be true, couldn't it? I know you, you see. I know that you are honest and true, that your soul is as beautiful as your body, and the way to win you is to make you believe that I am the same.

"Any man with his wits about him would come to you as I am doing, knowing that you would trust him for his frankness. It looks honest, you see. But a man who speaks ill of himself is sometimes telling the truth."

"Not you," she said at once. "You say you know me, but *I* know *you*. You are incapable of dishonour. If you say you love me, I will believe you."

"That is why I cannot say it," he told her bitterly. "How can we marry? Do you remember the words of the marriage service? '*With all my worldly goods I thee endow.*'"

"They are beautiful words."

"Yes, they are beautiful words, but how could *I* say them to *you*, Cliona? With what worldly goods shall I endow you? My debts? My crumbling house? My walls with their empty places where the pictures have been sold? My cousin, who will spend your fortune when he has finished with mine? Shall *he* be my wedding gift to you?"

"If you love me," she faltered, "I wouldn't care about anything else."

"How long would you believe that I love you, that I had married you for love?"

"I will believe what you tell me."

He looked at her in silence, tortured but determined.

"Oh I can't bear this," she cried. "You will break my heart for the sake of your pride."

"Cliona, please listen to me – "

"No, it is you who should listen. Without me you will

110

have to find another heiress. And then what will you do? Lie, and pretend to a love that you do not feel? Or tell her to her face that her money is all you want? Will either be more honourable than marrying a woman who loves you and whom you love?"

"I have not said I love you."

"But you do. I *know* you do." Her voice cracked with anguish. "And if you leave me now, you will condemn me to the others – the fortune hunting crowd who won't be frank with me, as you have been. You will abandon me to liars and deceivers."

"You will see through them," he said gently, "as you have before. And in the end you will find a better man and be glad that I let you go."

She had one further card to play. It was a dangerous one and she played it facing him defiantly.

"What happens if you don't find another woman with as much as you need?"

His temper began to flare.

"You are suggesting, I take it, that I should grab your fortune in case nothing better comes along? In other words, you think I am a cad."

"No, if you were a cad – or even a man of ordinary good sense – I wouldn't *have* to suggest it."

"By your definition a man of 'ordinary good sense' is a man with no self-respect. I can't behave as you think I ought to. I cannot grab like that. Not when it's you. You mean too much. You are worth better."

"Charles – don't throw away what we might have together from some mistaken notion of pride. Stop and think what you are doing, for both our sakes."

His face was like stone.

"I cannot be other than the man I am. If I could – "

She sighed. "If you could, I could not love you so much."

"I'll go now" said Charles. "But remember my warning. Stay clear of John."

The words seemed to trigger her anger. She stepped sharply back from him.

"You have no right to say that to me," she said proudly. "You have just severed all ties between us. Very well. I am free of you now, as you are free of me. I shall do as I please, and I shall see whoever I please."

"Cliona, be sensible. He's a bad man."

"Perhaps I think differently. You need no longer concern yourself with my affairs. Good day to you, Lord Hartley."

"Cliona!"

"Good day to you."

He had no choice but to give her a small, curt bow, and depart. He did not look back, so he did not see her run to the window and stand watching him until he was out of sight.

*

The day of the Merriton races was almost upon them, and Charles must give his whole attention to appearing as people expected, the proud owner of two racehorses, concerned that they should perform at their best, but otherwise without a care in the world.

The day would begin with the journey to the race track, five miles away. The ladies were to go by carriage, the men on horseback.

A horse-drawn fourgon would also travel, bearing servants and hampers with a chicken and champagne lunch.

The races were scheduled for the afternoon, after which certain honoured guests would stream back to Hartley

Castle for the ball that always ended the first day of the races.

In his agitation, Charles had almost forgotten the ball and would gladly have dispensed with it, had not his mother insisted.

"My dear Charles, the Hartley ball is a tradition. It is expected. Your father never missed a year, and neither must you. Besides, the invitations have already gone out."

"Good heavens! When?"

"Last week, as they always do. Really, you notice nothing these days."

There was one thing that Charles did notice, and that was John's daily absences. He would ride out in the morning and come back in the evening, a satisfied smile on his face.

Charles had even gone to the lengths of speaking to Sir Kenton, who knew the history of John's behaviour and strongly disapproved of him.

"I rely on you to forbid the match, sir," he said.

"Good lord, Charles, nobody's going to ask me if I agree or disagree. Cliona will become of age soon, so whatever I did they could set the wedding date for the day after her twenty first."

"You don't mean they are actually engaged?" asked Charles sharply.

"They could be for all I know. Cliona and Martha put their heads together, laughing and talking, but they don't tell me anything."

"But you know the truth about him," Charles exploded.

"Much good that does if a woman is in love. John can put himself out to be charming and Martha melts. Then she forgets what he is really like."

"And what does Lady Cliona say?" asked Charles, suddenly finding a spot on his boot that needed attention.

"Merely that he's delightful company and a good dancer. I caught them practising the waltz yesterday and she has promised him the first dance at the Hartley ball. They'll probably make an announcement there. Good place for it."

Charles rode home in a savage mood, and relayed the gist of this conversation to Freddy.

"How can she?" he fumed. "How can she allow him to lay a finger on her?"

"Perhaps she genuinely likes him," mused Freddy.

"Impossible!"

"Not impossible at all. Young girls have strange tastes. Look at the way she used to like you. That should show you."

"Are you ever serious?" Charles demanded scathingly.

"Not if I can avoid it. All right, here's a theory for you. John looks very like you. You're the one she wants, but she can't have you, so she makes do with him."

"Must you talk like a kitchen maid's novelette?" Charles demanded in disgust.

"Then how about this? She's trying to make you jealous."

"I've never heard such a disgraceful idea in my life," Charles snapped. "To suggest that she – even the thought that – let me tell you Freddy, that Lady Cliona is a young woman of the highest principles, who would scorn to descend to such methods. The mere idea of her indulging in cheap – "

"All right, all right, old fellow," said Freddy indulgently. "I get your drift." He wandered out through the French windows. "I'll say no more."

"I had to get away from Charles," he explained to

Cliona later that day, "or he would have gone on for hours, all about how you were above that sort of thing. He seemed to think I had insulted you, but I was simply admiring your tactics, ma'am."

"Strategy," she told him. "Tactics are for when the enemy can be seen and strategy is when the enemy is out of sight."

"But who's the enemy?"

"Charles of course. Oh, Freddy! Why do men never have any common sense?"

"Actually most of us do. But Charles is in love with you, so you can't expect it."

"I don't expect anything from him," she said crossly, "except bone-headed pride and a refusal to see what's under his nose."

Freddy nodded. "That sounds like him."

*

John had taken care to secure the position of Cliona's official escort to the races, and the entire Hartley party turned up together.

Lady Hester and the Countess were to take Sir Kenton and Lady Arnfield in their carriage. The gentlemen and Cliona would ride on horseback.

Charles had originally intended to go ahead to Merriton to make a last minute inspection of his horses, which had travelled two days earlier. But when the morning came he unaccountably changed his mind and rode with his family.

Within sight of the Kentons' house John urged his horse ahead, so that he arrived first and greeted Cliona.

The others were treated to the sight of him enclosing her hand between his own, as though he owned it.

Cliona looked charming in a riding habit of deep blue

velvet, with a lacy blouse and a fluttering feather in her hat, that drew attention to her enchanting face. She laughed at John's greeting and then turned her attention to the other gentlemen, holding out her hand impishly.

Freddy immediately seized it and kissed it outrageously. Charles occupied himself greeting the Arnfields. When he had finished, he gave Lady Cliona the briefest possible bow.

At last the party was ready to leave. The carriage turned out of the Arnfields' main gates, with the riders bringing up the rear, a bright and attractive party.

Cliona rode beside John, laughing and flirting with him. At last Charles said curtly,

"I should go on ahead to ensure that everything is ready for my guests. Your pardon, ma'am."

"I think Freddy should go too," declared John. "Off with you Freddy, we shan't miss you."

Freddy looked at Charles, wondering if he were really to leave the pair alone, but Charles nodded and galloped ahead, leaving Freddy no choice but to follow.

Cliona watched them go, refusing to allow the smile to fade from her face and also refusing to allow any doubts creep in. She had made her resolution and she would stick to it.

Her brand new riding habit had hung, unused, in the wardrobe since she had arrived. She had been saving it for a special occasion. The way it brought out the deep blue of her eyes, the snug fit on her pretty figure, were not to be wasted on ordinary days.

Now the special occasion had arrived. This was the day for the flowing skirt, the lacy blouse with the pearl at the throat and the neat jacket.

Last of all, the hat, perched jauntily over her left eye, with its cheeky feather, dancing as she moved her head.

Dressing that morning, she had felt like a General donning armour for battle. No battle in her life would ever be as important as the one she was fighting now. And her courage would not fail her.

Like any great warrior she knew when to risk everything. When Charles had come to see her the week before and blurted out his secret, instinct had told her that if she had persisted she could have dragged or tricked a proposal of marriage from him.

Then they would have married and because they loved each other, they would have been happy, after a fashion.

But it would have been a fatally flawed happiness.

A still deeper instinct had warned her not to take the easy path, that if he proposed to her in defiance of all that was best in him, there would be no peace in their marriage. She could not satisfy his heart at the expense of his pride, or only for a short time.

So she had stepped back, letting him go, hazarding everything for the chance of the greater prize.

Soon she would know whether she had thrown away her chance of happiness, or won the greatest glory of all.

So she rode on to whatever might be her destiny, with flags and pennants bravely fluttering and bugles that only she could hear.

CHAPTER NINE

Everyone agreed that the race meeting was a great success. Charles's horse had romped to victory in one race and the Lord Lieutenant's horse had won another. And in the last event of the day, a mile race for mares, they each had an entry.

Their friendly rivalry was the subject of much merriment. Sitting in Charles's box they drank champagne and planned their wagers.

"Naturally we shall place our money on my cousin's horse," said John to Cliona. "But perhaps we should wager on your uncle's as well. What is it called by the way?"

"Gina," said Cliona, reaching for her programme. "And his Lordship's horse is – " Her voice faded into silence.

Everyone in the box turned to look at her face, grown suddenly pale. Everyone for except Charles.

"What is it, my dear?" asked Sir Kenton.

"I renamed her at the last minute," Charles observed, looking bored. "A compliment to yourself, ma'am, since the mare is bound to win."

"Lady Cliona," said the Lord Lieutenant, reading from the programme. "Well, well!"

"I hope you don't feel I took too much of a liberty, sir,"

said Charles. "Since we are such old friends – "

"Of course, of course," Sir Kenton cried heartily. "Well, well! Cliona, do you see that?"

"Yes, sir," she said, laughing charmingly. "Lord Hartley flatters me."

She rose and faced Charles, dropping a little curtsy to him. "You are too kind to me, sir. But only consider, suppose my namesake loses?"

"I do not consider that a possibility," said Charles at once. "But if it happens, the blame will be all mine."

She regarded him, her head on one side.

"You are too quick to blame yourself," she said softly.

"On the contrary, ma'am. I believe a man should always be ready to take responsibility for his actions."

"But not for accidents over which he has no control," she pointed out. "A clever man should be able to tell the difference."

He did not answer, but looked at her sadly.

"How are you?" she whispered.

"I am well, I thank you, ma'am. I hope you are enjoying a pleasant day."

"Very much. The entertainment is excellent, and your cousin exerts himself endlessly on my behalf."

"I am glad to hear it," said Charles in a colourless voice. "Perhaps you will excuse me."

He inclined his head, and went to pay attention to a couple who had arrived to visit his box. Watkins bustled about with champagne.

"That settles it," said John, handing Cliona a full glass. "I will back Lady Cliona only to win the race."

"Poor Lady Cliona," she said, smiling. "To have everyone's eyes on her, all expecting something. I wonder if she will find the burden too much."

"Impossible! Her success is assured in everything she does," said John cheerfully. But then he saw a shadow on her face and hurried to say, "perhaps this kind of fooling is not to your taste. I beg your pardon. I talk nonsense because I cannot speak the things that are in my heart."

"A man should speak of what is in his heart," said Cliona, with a touch of fierceness. "It's when he ignores his heart and says what he thinks he ought to say that he gets everything wrong."

"Even if he says things he has no right to say?" asked John after a moment. He was feeling his way carefully, unable to believe his luck.

"If he truly means his words, then he has the right to say them," Cliona murmured.

"But I am a poor man."

"I have realised that."

"And wondered how I dared to seek you out, I dare say. I will be honest with you. I thought only of idle flirtation and I was sure that you too were merely amusing yourself, since all thought of – anything else – between us was impossible."

Cliona kept her head a little lowered. She did not want John to see her eyes, lest he read in them her disgust. It was unlucky for him that his words echoed those spoken to her by Charles in their last violent encounter.

How different it had all sounded from Charles, she thought.

John was speaking again.

"But now everything is changed. What started as flirtation has become love, and since you encourage me to speak my mind, I will tell you that I love you madly and my greatest joy would be to make you my wife. I care nothing for your fortune. Give it all away. But give yourself to me, that is all I ask."

He spoke smoothly and well, but it only had the effect of reminding her of another man, who spoke, not smoothly and well, but awkwardly from the heart.

"Shall I really give it all away?" she asked with a little smile.

"Only say that you will be my wife, and I ask no other gift," he said in a low, fervent voice.

Later such rash assertions could be taken back. He knew that her uncle would not permit her to give up a penny. In fact, as her fiancé he would have legal rights and could prevent it himself.

"You must give me a little time," she said modestly. "This is so sudden."

"How can it be? You must have known – " he checked himself before a flash of irritation could be his undoing.

"All the time you need," he said. "I am your servant, now and always. Only do not make me suffer too long. I long to take your hand in mine – " he seized her left hand and touched the wedding finger, "and place a ring on this dear finger."

"Be a little patient," she advised, withdrawing her hand.

He smiled and managed to suppress his impatience with her shilly-shallying. He felt too close to his goal to risk it by a false step now.

"Will you share a toast with me?" he asked. "To Lady Cliona and her success."

Solemnly they clinked their champagne glasses.

By now people in the other boxes were looking at them. News of the renamed mare had gone round the stadium, along with the information that Lady Cliona herself

121

was present. People raised their glasses to her.

Only Charles stood aloof, thunderstruck by what he had just witnessed. He had seen John and Cliona talking intently, gazing deep into each other's eyes. He had seen John take her left hand and single out the wedding finger.

Then they had toasted each other in champagne.

There could be no mistaking the meaning. They would make the announcement at the ball tonight.

Cold horror possessed him. He felt like a man who had suddenly found he was looking down into an abyss.

The mares were being paraded along the track to the starting line. There were eight of them, the third wearing the blue and yellow colours of the Lord Lieutenant, and the fourth in the green and white colours of the Earl of Hartley.

They lined up behind the tape. The starting pistol was fired and they were away.

For a few moments the horses were bunched, but then two moved out ahead of the rest. Gina and Lady Cliona. The crowd began to roar.

Neck and neck they took the first bend. Then into the back straight, still nothing in it, until Gina began to inch ahead, just a little, then a little more. She was a head clear as they came round the last bend.

In the box Sir Kenton and his lady were looking anxious, uncertain whether it was proper for them to cheer on their own animal or not. Cliona solved the problem for them by jumping to her feet and calling, "Come on, Gina! Come on, Gina!"

On the last bend Gina drew further ahead and it seemed that nothing could get between her and the winning post, but with two hundred yards to go Lady Cliona began to inch forward until they were level – a few more yards – the winning post was in sight.

A roar broke from the crowd as Lady Cliona just got her nose in front as they streaked across the line.

Now the real Cliona was the toast of the race track. All around people in the boxes cheered and waved, calling her name.

In the midst of this whirlwind she stood, accepting the tributes, apparently enjoying them, but inwardly thinking how different this might have been.

If it had been Charles who had asked her to marry him instead of John, this would have been a wonderful moment. True, he invited her to come with him to the winner's enclosure, but he invited the rest of the party too and did not encourage her to walk beside him.

For a brief moment she knew a chill of fear. Suppose she failed. Then she might look back on this as the moment when everything slipped through her grasp, and she was left contemplating a desolate future.

For a instant she forgot everything else. She became oblivious to those around her. It was like opening her eyes and discovering herself in the middle of winter. A winter that would last forever.

But then her courage returned. She raised her head, smiled and looked round her.

Charles was watching her. He had seen everything, including the momentary despair that she knew must have shown in her face.

But she would die sooner than ask for his pity. She smiled at him and slipped her hand into John's arm.

Charles turned away.

He did not join the cheerful party that drove home, galloping ahead on the pretext of seeing that all the preparations for the ball were in hand at the castle. In vain did his mother protest that this was her task and she had performed it very efficiently. He kissed her hand and departed with Freddy, leaving Cliona to ride home beside John in the setting sun.

*

At nine o'clock the guests started to arrive. Anyone looking out of an upper window would have seen a long stream of carriages making their way to the front door of Hartley Castle.

The Countess and Lady Hester were resplendent in diamonds and rubies (collected from the bank that morning) with a few ostrich feathers to add effect.

Charles, Freddy and John were all austerely handsome in white tie and tails, waiting in the entrance to the ballroom as the first guests appeared.

Lady Hester had outdone herself in the ballroom decorations, a symphony in silk and flowers. The orchestra was the best that the neighbourhood had to offer.

It had cost a fortune, Charles reflected. But Lady Hester had somehow convinced herself that all was now well, and he did not have the heart to disillusion her.

Ladies, dressed in their finest gowns and jewels, came sailing into the ballroom like gorgeous galleons. But none was as beautiful as Lady Cliona in white satin brocade draped over a huge crinoline.

Everyone knew that she was the richest woman present, yet cleverly she had chosen to wear no jewellery. Only flowers adorned her hair. Her neck and creamy shoulders were bare. She needed no other adornment. She was perfect in herself.

Her one extravagance was a huge white fan, made of frothy feathers and glittering with spangles.

She made a gracious curtsy to Charles, her host, but it was John who stepped forward to take her hand for the first dance. And a murmur went around the guests that it was only a matter of time before there was a happy announcement.

Somehow Charles got through the first dance with the daughter of the local Mayor. As soon as it was over, he sought out Cliona.

"I don't care whose name is written on your card," he said. "You will dance the next dance with me. I am, after all, your host."

"But of course," she said at once. "I kept the next dance for you for just that reason."

"Indeed?" he said, speaking more sharply than he had intended. "Suppose I had not asked you?"

She smiled. "You did not ask. You demanded."

"Will you dance with me, Cliona?"

"Gladly."

Like fairy dust she drifted into his arms. A soft fragrance floated up from her warm body, assailing his senses and making him giddy. Her lovely face was turned towards him, a gentle smile touching her lips. He tried not to look at those lips, lest the desire to kiss them should overcome him.

"What are you thinking?" she asked.

Against his will the words came out. "I am thinking that this is the last time we shall dance together."

"Why?"

"Because I will never dance with you when you are Mrs. John Baxter."

"Perhaps I never will be?"

"Stop it," he said furiously. "Whatever game you are playing, stop it."

"I'm not playing, Charles. This is deadly serious for me."

"Serious?" he said scathingly. "You expect me to take seriously a woman who – who – ?"

He could not think. Words tumbled about in his brain but everything was chaos. Only his senses spoke to him, and they told him to dance her out of the open French windows onto the wide terrace, sweep her around faster and faster until they were well away from the house.

There in the semi-darkness he could cast aside restraint and pull her into his arms for the kiss he had yearned for every night and day.

He kissed her with no regard to gentlemanly restraint, but fiercely, demandingly, as though they were the only man and woman in the world.

And now Cliona discovered what a truly perverse creature she was, for she too had yearned for his kiss. Yet now it had come, she found that her first ecstasy swiftly gave way to indignation.

This man had taken her to the heights and then rejected and insulted her. He had ordered her about, imposed his decisions on her and now he felt entitled to kiss her by force. Just who did he think he was?

"How dare you!" she cried, struggling free. "I will not be taken for granted by a man who's acting like a dog in the manger. You don't want me yourself but you won't let anyone else have me. But that is my decision – now let me go! What do you think you're doing?"

"Teaching you some sense," he growled, pulling her back into his arms. "Does he kiss you like this? If so, go ahead and marry him, but *does he?*"

There was a long silence as Cliona felt the strength drain out of her. If his arms had not been tight about her she would have fallen. Her heart was beating wildly and she could feel his strong heart beat against her. She wanted to stay like this forever, floating upwards in a dream where they would always be together.

At any moment he would say the words she longed to hear.

But the sound that broke the spell was not Charles's voice speaking of love, but something else. Something that froze her blood.

A small, polite cough.

Appalled, they both looked up to find John standing there.

He was smiling.

"I say, old fellow," he said amiably, "that's going a bit far, isn't it? Forcing your attentions on a lady! I could hear her tell you to let her go from half way down the terrace."

Charles was shaking with the passion that possessed him and from the effort to control himself. Somehow he managed to think clearly.

Forcing his attentions on a lady! Yes, that was it. Only in that way could her reputation be preserved. His face hardened and that was what she saw when she looked at him.

John strolled forward and took Cliona's hand as Charles stepped back.

"I guess I arrived just in time, my dear," he said smoothly. "No need to make a fuss. Charles doesn't mean anything by it. Devil of a ladies' man, you know."

He was leading her back along the terrace as he spoke and she went with him in a daze.

Now it was all over. Nothing could save her. She had misplayed her hand.

And what did it matter anyway? Charles did not want her enough to fight for her.

But as she walked she was praying desperately as she

had done before when things had seemed beyond hope.

'Please, please,' she whispered silently, 'let something happen. I don't know what. I can't think any more, I'm too confused. But throw me a lifeline – *please* – '

The guests now came spilling out onto the terrace, regarding them with wonder.

"So there you are," hooted the Countess. "We wondered where the three of you had got to."

Charles never knew how he replied. His head was spinning. He supposed he said something meaningless about the ball, refreshments, the next dance, anything.

"You should rejoin your guests," said the Countess. "It is time to – good heavens, what is that noise?"

A commotion was coming from the lawn just below, voices shouting, one voice shouting louder than the others, a determined bellow from a man who would not be denied.

"You shall not stop me. Out of my way."

"Sir, you cannot – "

"Out of my way!"

In the darkness they could just make out figures running across the lawn to the steps that led up to the terrace. The first one to reach them was a man of about sixty. He was wild in every way. His white hair was wild and standing up on his head. His clothes were wild, his face was wild. But most of all his eyes were wild.

Dark, mad eyes, burning with fever, with rage, with hate.

"My name is Jacob Ormerod," he said hoarsely, "And I have come to bring a thief to justice. "There he is!" he roared, pointing a shaking finger. "The cheat, the liar, the thief. He stole my home."

Servants had come stumbling up the steps after him and would have seized him, but Charles waved them back.

All eyes were on the madman, shaking with fury and then at the man he had singled out.

John.

John stood motionless but his eyes were almost as livid as his tormentor's. A thin smile played around his lips. He had confronted his victims before, but he preferred not to do it in public.

"Thief!" the intruder screamed. "He stole my home."

"It was your idea to stake your title deeds," said John coldly. "I was reluctant, but you insisted."

"It was my only way to win back what you had cheated from me," the man cried hoarsely.

"Be very careful," said John waspishly. "What you have just said is slander."

"What I have said is the truth."

"Did you win this man's home?" Charles demanded of John in a low voice.

"In a fair game, and it was his idea to stake his deeds. I was against it, for precisely this reason. They insist on high stakes and then they scream if they lose."

"For pity's sake, John, give it back."

"Are you out of your mind? This was my biggest stroke of luck in years."

"You should never have accepted the wager – "

"But I did, and I won it fair and square."

"Did you?" Charles asked coldly.

"What are you suggesting? That I cheated? Shame on you Charles. Think of the family."

Charles swore under his breath. He could not, under his own roof, accuse his cousin of cheating. If the club stewards had seen evidence of cheating, they would have intervened at the time.

And yet John had deprived a man of his home, and this was the result. The damage to the family name was as bad either way.

The man had staggered from the violence of his emotions and would have fallen, but some of the guests supported him while others led him to a stone seat. One of the women gave him a glass of wine.

John's mind was working fast on two tracks at once. He had behaved coolly when he found Cliona in his cousin's arms, hoping that by not antagonising her he might still reap the golden harvest that she represented.

Yet, at the same time, he knew that he had lost her. He was gambling on the chance of being able to claim her, even while he knew that chance to be almost non-existent.

He might have to return Ormerod's deeds, to impress Cliona. Yet another instinct told him to hold onto them, for he was going to need every penny for himself. And an odd twist in his nature forced him to play both parts at once.

Cliona was talking gently to the old man, holding his hand. After a while she rose and came across to where Charles and John were standing. To Charles's astonishment she was now laughing as though enjoying a joke.

"It is quite absurd," she said to John. "Mr. Ormerod seems to be under the impression that you carry the deeds on your person at all times and can hand them over now. How can he be so absurd? You will have left them in a bank in London."

"What a splendidly level-headed woman you are," he said admiringly. "That would, of course, have been the sensible thing to do, but I was reluctant to leave them."

Cliona clapped her hands. "You mean they are here in this house? Oh how clever! I should so like to see them."

He grinned at her, then lifted her chin with his fingers in a way that made Charles want to knock him down.

At the same time he was appalled by Cliona's

behaviour. How could this scatterbrained creature be the ethereal woman he thought he knew and loved?

John summoned one of the footmen, standing woodenly by the walls, pretending not to notice the drama going on.

"Find my valet, Raskin," he said, "and bring him here at once."

"John, for pity's sake!" Charles said as they waited. "Give him back his home."

"My home, I think, Charles. Legally mine now. That should please you. The sale should bring in quite a bit. Assuming, of course, that I don't find some other source of income in the meantime, which I rather think I will. That will please you too, I dare say."

"Keep your voice down," said Charles sharply, glancing at Cliona who, mercifully, did not seem to have heard.

John shrugged. "It'll be no secret soon. Ah, Raskin, here is the key to the special box. Fetch me the documents inside, and hurry."

Raskin hurried away. A hush had fallen over the crowd. Some were looking at Ormerod, some at John, all looked unsure how to react.

"Will you think carefully about what you're doing?" Charles urged John. "These people have started to like you. Will you wantonly throw away their goodwill now you have it?"

"My dear Charles," murmured John, "they may take their goodwill and do with it as they please. What do I care for their goodwill?"

Ormerod, slightly revived by a glass of wine was getting to his feet, his tired eyes alight with hope.

"You have sent for the deeds? You will return them to

me. I beg you – my family will be destitute – I beg you – let me have them back."

"Perhaps I will," John mused. "We will see what happens."

"But you must – you must – " Ormerod pleaded. "I am going mad – it's a sickness, the gambling – it comes over me – and then I don't know what I'm doing – "

Charles gently took hold of him and led him to a seat, where Ormerod half fell and dropped his head into his hands. Cliona was standing nearby and Charles drew her aside.

"I don't know if you have any influence over that cruel man," he said. "But if you have, for pity's sake use it."

"He goes his own way," she said in an edgy voice. "He won't give in without getting something in return."

"If he loves you, he will. Ask him, flatter him, implore him. Get those deeds back."

She gave him a direct look. "Is this what *you* want?"

He did not answer. There were no words to tell her what he wanted.

Raskin had returned with the deeds. Ormerod's eyes brightened and he made a futile lunge for them, but John stepped quickly back, thrusting the deeds into his inner coat pocket.

"You said you would give them to me," Ormerod screamed.

"No, I said perhaps," John told him coldly. "I will make you a proposition, Mr. Ormerod. You lost these deeds at gaming. I'll play you for them again. And to show my good intentions, I shall not ask any stake from you. I stand to lose the deeds. You stand to lose nothing."

A relaxed murmur went round the crowd for they all thought they knew what John had in mind. He would let Ormerod win, and so return the deeds while allowing the old man to recover some dignity.

But Charles was unconvinced. He knew John better than to expect any act of kindness. He was playing with Ormerod, amusing himself with the man's grief. And he would humiliate him for more amusement.

Ormerod had to have everything explained to him twice. He looked half dead with weariness, and as if he had not eaten for days and Charles was certain that he was in no mental condition to play a game of cards. He would have liked to stop this charade but he could not deny the poor man the chance to redeem his deeds, however slight a chance it might be.

Ormerod finally raised his head and seemed to give himself a shake.

"What are we to play?" he asked with a touch of defiance.

"Poker," said John.

People looked at each other. Many had never heard of the game. Few knew how it was played.

"It's what we were playing that night," said John. "So we must play the same game now."

Cliona was standing near to Charles. "They play it a lot in America," she said. "Papa told me. As a young man he once took a trip on a riverboat along the Mississippi. He was on the boat for weeks, winning and losing. It's known as 'the cheating game'."

"Then John will cheat," groaned Charles.

"He probably cheated that night," observed the Lord Lieutenant. "Perhaps he can only be defeated by someone with the same skills."

"And I doubt Ormerod has them. But it makes no odds. This is his only chance."

A small table was brought out for the players. Because the night was warm and the ballroom growing uncomfortably hot, the table was set out on the terrace, but near to the light.

Now that the decision had been made, Ormerod was calm. Freddy began explaining the rules to the spectators.

"It's really a game of bluff," he said. "Each player is dealt a hand of cards and then they raise the stakes if they think they have a good enough hand. The trick is to guess how good the other fellow's hand is and pretend that yours is better than it is. You can improve your hand by changing cards."

"Very well," said Charles grimly. "If we are doing this, we'll do it properly. Sir," this to Sir Kenton, "as Lord Lieutenant, will you take charge of the deeds, and award them to the rightful owner when the game is over?"

"Certainly," agreed Sir Kenton.

The players faced each other over the table. Freddy dealt the cards and they each raised their hand.

At once it became obvious that Ormerod could never compete. He added to his hand, discarded some cards, but seemed to do so without rhyme or reason. At last John laid his cards on the table. He had four queens. Only four kings or four aces would outdo them.

Ormerod had a three, a five, and two sevens.

"My hand, I think," said John.

Ormerod moaned.

"Stop this," said Charles sharply. "Stop tormenting the poor man."

"But I am offering him another chance," said John. "I'm willing to play another hand. Will you deny him the chance?"

There was the catch. Any attempt that Charles made to protect Ormerod could deny him his last chance.

Ormerod knew it too.

"Another hand," he cried. "I'll win this one."

"But you are not well, sir," came a sweet voice. The speaker was Lady Cliona.

"You are unwell", she repeated. "Let someone else take your place."

The gentlemen looked at each other, aghast. Who could take on such a heavy responsibility?

"Then I will play for you," said Cliona, smiling at him. "I know this game well."

Ormerod rose to his feet, remembering that he had once been a gallant gentleman.

"Too kind – this game is not for ladies – "

Cliona laughed. "Never fear, sir. I am not like other ladies. I play poker very well."

"As well as me?" John asked with a faint sneer.

Cliona answered him strangely. "I play the same game that you do, sir."

"Not a game for ladies – " Ormerod repeated. Then he swayed and had to be caught.

Cliona seated herself firmly in his place. Charles came to her quickly.

"Cliona, listen – "

"The poor man has nothing to lose," she said unanswerably.

"But suppose I do not agree?" asked John. "Why should I? What do I have to gain?"

"What do you want to gain?" asked Cliona.

"You know what I want, ma'am."

Cliona smiled.

"Very well, then. Mr. Baxter, earlier today you asked me a question, to which I have not yet given you an answer. I answer you now. If you win this game, I will marry you."

CHAPTER TEN

"No!"

There was a general murmur of disapproval, but Charles's cry could be heard over all the rest.

"No!" he said again. "I forbid it."

"You have no power to forbid it," retorted John. "Mind your own business, Charles."

"Cliona," he tried to take hold of her, "for pity's sake stop this. You cannot do it. Just stop and think what you could do to us?"

"Us?" she whispered so that only he could hear. "Is there such a thing?"

"I will do anything you want," Charles cried. "I'll give in."

"I don't want you to give in. I wanted you to come to me willingly and with a full heart. But you did not want to do that. Now I insist on my right to bestow my hand where I please."

With horror he realised that she was implacable. This girl who looked so frail had an inner core of steel. She was stronger than anyone. Perhaps she was even stronger than him.

But was she stronger than John?

It was hard to believe that she could be, as she sat there

gently fanning herself with her outrageous feather fan.

The game proceeded despite Charles.

Once more Freddy dealt the cards. Cliona took a quick look at her hand, then held it against her chest, so that it was concealed from everyone else. Her face appeared calm.

Charles moved to stand behind John, in order to get a better view of Cliona.

At this very moment she held their future in her hands and only she knew what that might be.

Charles raised his eyes to the heavens, high and dark above them. Such a terrible, icy indifference he thought.

And then he saw his star.

It sparkled and glittered, outshining any other star. It was his. She had given it to him and it would be his forever.

His lucky star, she had told him. But could it help them now?

She played with quiet concentration, taking up and discarding cards. John seemed confident, too confident, Charles thought. He changed cards, but not as often as Cliona, and he repeatedly asked her if she was ready to show her hand. Always she refused, and Charles began to get a sick, apprehensive feeling in his stomach as he realised that she did not know what to do.

But *he* knew what to do. He knew, because she had told him, when they had first met, before he had spoiled their love with his pride and confusion.

He began to pray. But the prayer he uttered was not for himself.

'Save her,' he prayed silently. 'Never mind me. Save and protect *her*.'

At almost the same moment she spoke.

"I will see your hand, sir."

A cold smile overtook John's face as he laid his cards

137

face up on the table and a gasp of horror surged through the guests.

Four queens.

Exactly the same as before.

No man could honestly achieve that hand twice running. In some way that nobody had noticed, he had cheated.

Charles wanted to howl to the star above that it had failed him. How could it have let Cliona walk into such a fool's trap?

In total silence she raised her eyes to meet Charles's. Their eyes held for a long moment.

John spoke,

"Well? Can you match my queens with kings?"

At last Cliona looked away from Charles towards John. It was as though a warrior had taken up his spear and shield and marched out of the tent. Now only the battle counted.

"No, sir," she said. "I cannot."

A long sigh came from everyone around the table. To the last moment Charles had clung to a faint hope. But at these words he felt his world begin to crumble.

Without taking her eyes from her opponent, Cliona laid her cards on the table.

Four aces.

A cheer broke out.

Now she raised her head to look at Charles again, sending him a silent message. In the midst of the noisy, rejoicing room, only the two of them existed. And something had happened that only they understood.

John's face grew livid as the truth dawned on him. He rose sharply and lunged at Sir Kenton in an attempt to retrieve the deeds. Sir Kenton closed his hands over his coat, but it was unnecessary. At least three men had intervened between him and John.

Cliona rose and confronted John.

"You have lost, sir," she said coldly. "The deeds you staked now belong to Mr. Ormerod."

"It's a trick," John raged. "You cheated."

Uproar! To accuse a lady of cheating! But Cliona remained unruffled.

"I told you, I play the same game as you," she reminded John. "Do you cheat?"

He did not answer. He could not. All around him were accusing eyes.

"Uncle, may I have Mr. Ormerod's property, please?" Cliona asked the Lord Lieutenant.

"Certainly, my dear." Sir Kenton reached into his coat for the deeds, which he handed to Cliona.

But instead of giving them to Mr. Ormerod, she turned to Charles, speaking loudly so that all might hear.

"My Lord, will you allow Mr. Ormerod to remain here for the night?"

"It was my intention to do so, ma'am," he replied.

"And will you instruct a man to sleep in the room with him, and another man to stand on guard outside his door?"

"Perhaps two strong men will be needed to stand outside," he said, understanding her. "What is your opinion?"

"I agree. May I further request that two – no four – men accompany Mr. Ormerod when he leaves tomorrow?"

"Four men will be better," said Charles with a pointed glance at John. "One never knows what accidents may befall on a journey."

"And then these men can accompany Mr. Ormerod to

his home, where they will see these – " Cliona held up the deeds, "deposited in a safe place."

Charles nodded. "In some bank or a lawyer's office."

Cliona shook her head. "No, I meant they should be put into the hands of Mrs. Ormerod."

"You are entirely right, ma'am," said Charles. "Let us hope that from now on, his wife can keep him in order."

"Every man needs a wife to do that," Cliona pointed out.

"Whatever you say. I bow to your superior knowledge. In fact, right this minute, I feel inclined to entrust my entire future into your hands, knowing that they are safer than my own." He smiled. "Because you are far, far wiser than I."

"That is true," she told him severely. "And I hope you will never forget it."

He took her hand in his. "I doubt if I shall ever be allowed to," he said fondly. He lowered his voice. "Cliona, can we leave this room and be alone somewhere? I badly need to kiss you."

"I think we should make the announcement first."

"Must we?"

"Yes, I want to make sure of you before you think up some other problem that doesn't matter."

"But can't we just – ? Oh, the devil!"

Before she could speak he swept her up into his arms, kissing her fiercely while their guests cheered and clapped.

Only one person was not joyful. John regarded them with stony eyes. Then he turned on his heel and walked out. Nobody watched him go.

Charles kissed his beloved until they were both breathless. Then he took firm hold of her and ran down the steps, across the lawn and into the trees. There, shielded by darkness, he drew her into his arms again.

"You are mine," he breathed. "You have been mine from the first moment – "

"Yes – yes – " she cried eagerly.

"And you will always been mine. Until the end of time."

"Yes," she cried again, and the word was cut off by his lips.

"I love you so much," he declared when he could speak again. "Why was I such a fool as to think anything else mattered? Can you forgive me, my darling?"

"There's nothing to forgive," she said ecstatically. "As long as you love me."

"I shall always love you. Tonight I thought I might lose you forever. How could you take such a risk, my beloved?"

"But I had to. It was the miracle I asked for. After John found us together I was praying for something to happen, something I could do to make things turn out right.

"And then Ormerod arrived," she continued "and I knew that he was the answer to my prayer. I didn't know how, but I was certain that if I waited for the moment, it would come. And it did."

She put her hands on either side of his face.

"And then a strange thing happened, my darling. You were standing opposite me and I saw you look up into the sky."

"I was looking at the star you gave me."

"No, it was always yours."

"But I didn't know about it until *you* gave it to me. And I thought perhaps it might really be able to help us. I prayed that you might be protected."

She nodded wisely.

"That explains it."

"Explains what, my dearest?"

"The sensation I felt that you were holding my hand. It was quite illogical, because I was using both hands for my cards. But I felt it just the same. Do you understand that?"

"I do now. I might not have done before I met you. You have shown me so many things, so many wonders in this world that I did not know. But the greatest wonder of all is you."

He drew her close again and for a long time there was silence.

"We must be married very soon," he said at last.

"Very soon," she agreed. "And now I suppose we should go back to your guests and do everything the proper way."

"Let us walk slowly then, because there is still something I want to ask you."

"What is that?"

"How did you do it? How did you manage to draw four aces?"

"I just remembered all the things Papa taught me – keep your head, read your opponent, don't let him read you. It's all common sense really."

"Common sense didn't give you those aces. Did your Papa's lessons happen to include cheating at cards?"

She became prim. "Please, Charles. Where I come from, it isn't called cheating. It's called making the most of your opportunities."

"And I dare say a large, feathered fan is useful for 'making the most of your opportunities'?"

"Well Papa never used one," Cliona countered innocently.

He gave a choke of laughter.

"Mind you," she continued, "gentlemen have sleeves."

"You are not going to tell me the answer, are you?"

Smiling, she laid her fingertips against his lips.

"There are some things no lady should admit to knowing," she said.

*

The *King's Head* tavern lay at the end of the meanest street in London, overlooking the river. It was frequented by sailors and by ruffians who slept most of the day and who were for hire for almost anything.

Raskin who was picking his way through the smoke filled atmosphere, finally found the man he had come to meet, sitting in a corner, alone, his small eyes searching the gloom.

Raskin slid onto the wooden bench beside him.

"Thought you weren't coming," the man, whose name was Preece, grunted.

"I'm here now."

"Got the money?"

"Half. The rest when you've done a good job."

"Wait a minute, not so fast. First I want to meet him."

"Meet who?"

"The man who's hiring me to – "

"Shut your mouth," said Raskin, looking round, terrified. "Do you want to get us all caught?"

"To do this job," snapped Preece. "A job like this – being special – I like to meet who I'm working for."

After a moment Raskin nodded and rose. "All right. Follow me."

It took a few minutes for them to get out into the cool night air. Then Raskin strode ahead for a few streets until they came to a plain closed carriage standing by the road.

"Get in," he said.

Preece did so and found himself in near darkness. He could barely make out the other man, sitting opposite him, but he heard his cold voice.

"You know what you have to do?"

"The other bloke explained it to me," said Preece.

"And the money has been agreed?"

"Well – I could do with a bit more."

"You'll get the agreed price. You villains can be bought for ten a penny on any street corner."

Preece snickered. "Not many can shoot as straight as I can."

"I have only your word for that. But there will be a bonus if you kill him with one shot, straight through the heart."

"Understood."

"Don't let me down."

"What's this bloke done to you?"

The voice from the corner of the carriage was like a blast of ice.

"He has taken everything from me, my inheritance and the woman who should have been mine. I want to watch him die. On his wedding day. Now leave. You will be contacted with the final arrangements."

Preece was glad to go. There was something about this man that froze his blood.

When he was alone, John sat very still for a long time, trying to silence the tempests in his head.

At last he struck a match and by its light he read again the letter from Charles that he had received that morning.

"Both Cliona and I hope to see you at our wedding and that some way can be found for us to be cordial in the

future. But I must make it clear that there will be no more money. You have thrown away much of my fortune, but you will not do the same with hers."

John put the match to the letter and watched it burn. His face was livid in the flames.

"On his wedding day," he murmured. "And I shall be there to see it."

*

Both bride and groom were eager to marry as soon as possible, so the date was set for the following month, when the weather would still be good enough for the wedding feast to be held outdoors.

Lady Hester and the Countess plunged into a whirl of preparations, eagerly assisted by Lady Arnfield. Soon the castle gleamed in readiness for the new Countess.

Freddy was to be the best man. Charles did not feel that he could ask John to perform this office, although he did insist on inviting him.

To everyone's surprise John wrote back a civil acceptance that contained no hint of resentment at having his income cut off. Indeed, he did not even mention it.

It was Charles's delight in those days to show his darling around the estate that she would soon share with him. And one evening, when they were strolling on the terrace, he broached something that had long been on his mind.

"Dearest," he started, "now that there are to be no secrets between us, I have a confession to make – a confession of a somewhat scandalous nature."

Wide-eyed, she gazed at him.

"The day after we met, I returned to the river. You were there, swimming."

She gasped.

"And you looked at me – while I was in a state of – "

145

she averted her eyes modestly, " – of undress. Without telling me you were there?"

He nodded. "I spied on you. I feel very ashamed. I feel even more ashamed of the fact that I thoroughly enjoyed every minute."

To his amazement and relief, Cliona chuckled.

"Did you like my ankles?"

"Very much."

"So I should hope, after the trouble I took to give you a good view of them."

"What – what did you say?"

"That's why I hopped onto the rock, so that you could see all of me."

"You mean – you knew I was there?"

"All the time."

"You knew you were being watched – ?"

"Spied on," she reminded him cheekily.

"By a man, who didn't even have the decency to show himself – "

"Yes, I can't tell you how annoyed I was that you went away without getting into your bathing suit too."

He tried again. "You deliberately revealed yourself to male eyes – ?"

"Only yours, my darling. It did seem such a shame not to let you see my figure. Oh dear!" she placed both her hands in his. "I am shameless, aren't I? Are you very disappointed in me?"

His lips twitched. "I am shocked," he informed her. "Shocked!"

"Do you think you can ever forgive me?"

He tightened his hands on hers. "Certainly I forgive you, my love." His eyes gleamed with amusement. "But only for the sake of your fortune, of course."

Watkins, the butler, happening to turn the corner of the house at that moment, was greeted by the astonishing sight of the Earl and the future Countess, locked in each other's arms and, as he later informed Mrs. Watkins, "laughing like a couple of mad creatures."

*

The day of the wedding dawned, warm and sunny as everyone had hoped. The castle was filled with almost every member of the Hartley family. John had arrived the night before, but so late that there had been no time for more than a brief greeting before he retired to bed. In the morning, however, Freddy reported that his mood seemed civil.

"I say 'seemed' because there's a look in his eye that I don't like," he told Charles. "He's on edge about something."

"That's natural," observed Charles, who was dressing. "Stop worrying, and start enjoying yourself, Freddy. Have you got the ring?"

"That's the fifth time you've asked. *You* stop worrying."

In the Lord Lieutenant's house the bride was putting the final touches to her wedding dress of snowy white satin, trimmed with lace.

Her long veil reached the floor and was held in place by a diamond tiara of fabulous value. And about her neck she wore Charles's wedding gift, a diamond pendant in the shape of a star.

This was an occasion for the village as well as the castle and they all turned out to watch the open carriage travelling to the little parish church. They had feared the wedding would take place in the castle chapel, but Cliona wanted everyone to share her happiness.

As she walked down the aisle on the arm of her uncle, she knew that the Heaven she had dreamed of was very near.

Charles was there, watching her approach, his heart in his eyes. And when he made his vows, claiming Cliona as his wife, he did so in a firm voice, so that the whole world should know.

The bells rang out joyfully as they came out into the sunshine, arm in arm, to the cheers of all their friends.

There were more cheers along the route to the castle. The people from the village loved Cliona for herself, but they also knew that she had brought prosperity with her. And they would all share it.

Tables covered in white linen were set out under the trees. Servants scurried back and forth with champagne. There were three wedding cakes so that there would be enough for everybody.

Charles was serenely happy, now that Cliona was his at last. He was longing to have her all to himself, but he was content to wait, watch and admire her.

In truth he was a little troubled by John. As Freddy had said, John seemed on edge and everything he did seemed slightly forced. It was, of course, natural that he should be a little uneasy. And yet Charles was assailed by the sense that something was wrong.

"All right, old man?" he said, coming to where John stood alone. "I can't tell you how glad I am that you came."

He drew him aside so that they could walk together.

John gave a wan smile. Looking into his eyes, Charles was shocked by what he saw. Not anger or hate, but a crushing misery, as of a soul in torment.

"I'm surprised that you wanted me to come," said John.

"It would not have been the same without you. We are

still family, and I don't forget the old days. I am sure you don't forget them either."

John seemed to be seeing everything through a dark mist. Voices reached him from a distance. A hard stone had settled in his breast, growing heavier by the minute.

But soon all this would be over. Just a few yards away, high in an oak tree, concealed by leaves, was the killer, his gun at the ready. He had lived for this, and at any moment –

"Come and join the party," said Charles, walking a few steps ahead and looking back.

He had stopped directly in the line of fire. As he raised his hand to beckon to his cousin, John thought of the gun, being raised at this very moment, pointed straight at Charles's head –

"No!" he screamed, launching himself forward violently.

He collided with Charles in the last split second before the gun fired. Then the two men were lying on the ground while screams rose all around them.

Preece, caught off balance by the recoil, fell out of the tree and was caught by the men beneath. But few had time to notice. Their eyes were turned to where Charles and John lay.

Cliona felt her heart stop at the sight of the man who had so recently become her husband. She pressed her hands over her mouth to stifle a scream.

But all was well. He was moving, getting up on one knee, unhurt.

It was John who lay still on the ground, an ugly red stain spreading over his white shirt.

"John," called Charles urgently. "For God's sake! John! *Get a doctor.*"

"No use, old man," John murmured. "Let it be. Just – talk to me – for a moment."

The darkness in his soul had cleared now and he could see Charles's face, full of the affection they had shared long ago. Then he felt himself being gathered up into his cousin's arms.

"It was – meant for you – " he murmured. "But then – I couldn't let it happen."

"You saved me," said Charles quietly. "Whatever you meant to do at the start, you saved my life."

"Glad of that. I don't know – what came over me. All these years – I was mad – "

"Yes," said Charles huskily. "You were not yourself. I always knew that. Hold on, John. The doctor will be here soon. He'll make you well, and it will be like old times again."

"No – it's best this way. As long as – things are all right between us – now."

"Yes," sighed Charles softly. "Things are all right between us, John. *John!*"

Nobody answered him. John's face showed the greyness of death and his silence was final.

With a heavy heart Charles laid his cousin's body on the grass. Rising to his feet he sought Cliona. She opened her arms to him and he rushed to her, to the only refuge his heart could desire.

*

Midnight. The castle was dark and silent. The guests had all gone. The officers of the law had gone. Preece was in a police cell to be conveyed to a larger prison the next day.

The bride and groom stood at the window, looking out over the peaceful land.

"I am so sorry the day was spoiled for you," Charles murmured.

She gave him the gentle smile he loved.

"I married you for better, for worse, my love" Cliona replied. "It is not just one day, but all the loving, wonderful years we will share in the future. At least we were together for what happened, and I pray that we will always be together, through any trouble."

"No trouble can be too great while I have you," he sighed. "I said you were wiser than I, and I meant it. Take my hand and lead me through the world, my beloved. For without you, all the roads lead nowhere."

He drew her close in a kiss that was a promise for the years to come, of trust and tenderness as well as passion. This woman was more than the centre of his world. She *was* his world.

And when this world was done, there was another world, even more beautiful because there they could never be parted.

He raised his eyes to the sky and saw what he was looking for.

One star, outshining every other. The star that had been her gift to him, along with so many other wonderful gifts.

The star that would always shine for them.